The Moon Endureth

John Buchan

I

"Qu'est-c'qui passe ici si tard, Compagnons de la Marjolaine,"

-CHANSONS DE FRANCE

...I came down from the mountain and into the pleasing valley of the Adige in as pelting a heat as ever mortal suffered under. The way underfoot was parched and white; I had newly come out of a wilderness of white limestone crags, and a sun of Italy blazed blindingly in an azure Italian sky. You are to suppose, my dear aunt, that I had had enough and something more of my craze for foot-marching. A fortnight ago I had gone to Belluno in a post-chaise, dismissed my fellow to carry my baggage by way of Verona, and with no more than a valise on my back plunged into the fastnesses of those mountains. I had a fancy to see the little sculptured hills which made backgrounds for Gianbellini, and there were rumours of great mountains built wholly of marble which shone like the battlements.

...1 This extract from the unpublished papers of the Manorwater family has seemed to the Editor worth printing for its historical interest. The famous Lady Molly Carteron became Countess of Manorwater by her second marriage. She was a wit and a friend of wits, and her nephew, the Honourable Charles Hervey-Townshend (afterwards our Ambassador at The Hague), addressed to her a series of amusing letters while making, after the fashion of his contemporaries, the Grand Tour of Europe. Three letters, written at various places in the Eastern Alps and despatched from Venice, contain the following short narrative....

of the Celestial City. So at any rate reported young Mr. Wyndham, who had travelled with me from Milan to Venice. I lay the first night at Pieve, where Titian had the fortune to be born, and the landlord at the inn displayed a set of villainous daubs which he swore were the early works of that master. Thence up a toilsome valley I journeyed to the Ampezzan country, valley where indeed I saw my white mountains, but, alas! no longer Celestial. For it rained like Westmorland for five endless days, while I kicked my heels in an inn and turned a canto of Aristo into halting English couplets. By-and-by it cleared, and I headed westward towards Bozen, among the tangle of rocks where the Dwarf King had once his rose-garden. The first night I had no inn but slept in the vile cabin of a forester, who spoke a tongue half Latin, half Dutch, which I failed to master. The next day was a blaze of heat, the mountain-paths lay thick with dust, and I had no wine from sunrise to sunset. Can you wonder that, when the following noon I saw Santa Chiara sleeping in its green circlet of meadows, my thought was only of a deep draught and a cool chamber? I protest that I am a great lover of natural beauty, of rock and cascade, and all the properties of the poet: but the enthusiasm of Rousseau himself would sink from the stars to earth if he had marched since breakfast in a cloud of dust with a throat like the nether millstone.

Yet I had not entered the place before Romance revived. The little town--a mere wayside halting-place on the great mountain-road to the North--had the air of mystery which foretells adventure. Why is it that a dwelling or a countenance catches the fancy with the promise of some strange destiny? I have houses in my mind which I know will some day and somehow be intertwined oddly with my life; and I have faces in memory of which I know nothing--save that I shall undoubtedly cast eyes again upon them. My first glimpses of Santa Chiara gave me this earnest of romance. It was walled and fortified, the streets were narrow pits of shade, old tenements with bent fronts swayed to meet each other. Melons lay drying on flat roofs, and yet now and then would come a high-pitched northern gable. Latin and Teuton met and mingled in the place, and, as Mr. Gibbon has taught us, the offspring of this admixture is something fantastic and unpredictable. I forgot my grievous thirst and my tired feet in admiration and a certain vague expectation of wonders. Here, ran my thought, it is fated, maybe, that romance and I shall at last compass a meeting. Perchance some princess is in need of my arm, or some affair of high policy is afoot in this jumble of old masonry. You will laugh at my folly, but I had an excuse for it. A fortnight in strange mountains disposes a man to look for something at his next encounter with his kind, and the sight of Santa Chiara would have fired the imagination of a judge in Chancery.

I strode happily into the courtyard of the Tre Croci, and presently had my expectation confirmed for I found my fellow,--a faithful rogue I got in

Rome on a Cardinal's recommendation,--hot in dispute with a lady's maid. The woman was old, harsh-featured--no Italian clearly, though she spoke fluently in the tongue. She rated my man like a pickpocket, and the dispute was over a room.

"The signor will bear me out," said Gianbattista. "Was not I sent to Verona with his baggage, and thence to this place of ill manners? Was I not bidden engage for him a suite of apartments? Did I not duly choose these fronting on the gallery, and dispose therein the signor's baggage? And lo! an hour ago I found it all turned into the yard and this woman installed in its place. It is monstrous, unbearable! Is this an inn for travellers, or haply the private mansion of these Magnificences?"

"My servant speaks truly," I said firmly yet with courtesy, having no mind to spoil adventure by urging rights. "He had orders to take these rooms for me, and I know not what higher power can countermand me."

The woman had been staring at me scornfully, for no doubt in my dusty habit I was a figure of small count; but at the sound of my voice she started, and cried out, "You are English, signor?"

I bowed an admission. "Then my mistress shall speak with you," she said, and dived into the inn like an elderly rabbit.

Gianbattista was for sending for the landlord and making a riot in that hostelry; but I stayed him, and bidding him fetch me a flask of white wine, three lemons, and a glass of eau de vie, I sat down peaceably at one of the little tables in the courtyard and prepared for the quenching of my thirst. Presently, as I sat drinking that excellent compound of my own invention, my shoulder was touched, and I turned to find the maid and her mistress. Alas for my hopes of a glorious being, young and lissom and bright with the warm riches of the south! I saw a short, stout little lady, well on the wrong side of thirty. She had plump red cheeks, and fair hair dressed indifferently in the Roman fashion. Two candid blue eyes redeemed her plainness, and a certain grave and gentle dignity. She was notably a gentlewoman, so I got up, doffed my hat, and awaited her commands.

She spoke in Italian. "Your pardon, signor, but I fear my good Cristine has done you unwittingly a wrong."

Cristine snorted at this premature plea of guilty, while I hastened to assure the fair apologist that any rooms I might have taken were freely at her service.

I spoke unconsciously in English, and she replied in a halting parody of that tongue. "I understand him," she said, "but I do not speak him happily. I will discourse, if the signor pleases, in our first speech."

She and her father, it appeared, had come over the Brenner, and arrived that morning at the Tre Croci, where they purposed to lie for some days. He was an old man, very feeble, and much depending upon her constant care. Wherefore it was necessary that the rooms of all the party should adjoin, and there was no suite of the size in the inn save that which I had taken. Would I therefore consent to forgo my right, and place her under an eternal debt?

I agreed most readily, being at all times careless where I sleep, so the bed be clean, or where I eat, so the meal be good. I bade my servant see the landlord and have my belongings carried to other rooms. Madame thanked me sweetly, and would have gone, when a thought detained her.

"It is but courteous," she said, "that you should know the names of those whom you have befriended. My father is called the Count d'Albani, and I am his only daughter. We travel to Florence, where we have a villa in the environs."

"My name," said I, "is Hervey-Townshend, an Englishman travelling abroad for his entertainment."

"Hervey?" she repeated. "Are you one of the family of Miladi Hervey?"

"My worthy aunt," I replied, with a tender recollection of that preposterous woman.

Madame turned to Cristine, and spoke rapidly in a whisper.

"My father, sir," she said, addressing me, "is an old frail man, little used to the company of strangers; but in former days he has had kindness from members of your house, and it would be a satisfaction to him, I think, to have the privilege of your acquaintance."

She spoke with the air of a vizier who promises a traveller a sight of the Grand Turk. I murmured my gratitude, and hastened after Gianbattista.

In an hour I had bathed, rid myself of my beard, and arrayed myself in decent clothing. Then I strolled out to inspect the little city, admired an altar-piece, chaffered with a Jew for a cameo, purchased some small necessaries, and returned early in the afternoon with a noble appetite for dinner.

The Tre Croci had been in happier days a Bishop's lodging, and possessed a dining-hall ceiled with black oak and adorned with frescos. It was used as a general salle a manger for all dwellers in the inn, and there accordingly I sat down to my long-deferred meal. At first there were no other diners, and I had two maids, as well as Gianbattista, to attend on my wants. Presently Madame d'Albani entered, escorted by Cristine and by a tall gaunt serving-man, who seemed no part of the hostelry. The landlord followed, bowing civilly, and the two women seated themselves at the little table at the farther end. "Il Signor Conte dines in his room," said Madame to the host, who withdrew to see to that gentleman's needs.

I found my eyes straying often to the little party in the cool twilight of that refectory. The man-servant was so old and battered, and of such a dignity, that he lent a touch of intrigue to the thing. He stood stiffly behind Madame's chair, handing dishes with an air of great reverence-- the lackey of a great noble, if I had ever seen the type. Madame never glanced toward me, but conversed sparingly with Cristine, while she pecked delicately at her food. Her name ran in my head with a tantalizing flavour of the familiar. Albani! D'Albani! It was a name not uncommon in the Roman States, but I had never heard it linked to a noble family. And yet I had somehow, somewhere; and in the vain effort at recollection I had almost forgotten my hunger. There was nothing bourgeois in the little lady. The austere servants, the high manner of condescension, spake of a stock used to deference, though, maybe, pitifully decayed in its fortunes. There was a mystery in these quiet folk which tickled my curiosity. Romance after all was not destined to fail me at Santa Chiara.

My doings of the afternoon were of interest to me alone. Suffice it to say that when at nightfall I found Gianbattista the trustee of a letter. It was from Madame, written in a fine thin hand on a delicate paper, and it invited me to wait upon the signor her father, that evening at eight o'clock. What caught my eye was a coronet stamped in a corner. A coronet, I say, but in truth it was a crown, the same as surmounts the Arms Royal of England on the sign-board of a Court tradesman. I marvelled at the ways of foreign heraldry. Either this family of d'Albani had higher pretensions than I had given it credit for, or it employed an unlearned and imaginative stationer. I scribbled a line of acceptance and went to dress.

The hour of eight found me knocking at the Count's door. The grim serving-man admitted me to the pleasant chamber which should have been mine own. A dozen wax candles burned in sconces, and on the table among fruits and the remains of supper stood a handsome candelabra of silver. A small fire of logs had been lit on the hearth, and before it in an armchair sat a strange figure of a man. He seemed not so much old as aged. I should have put him at sixty, but the marks he bore were clearly less those of time than of life. There sprawled before me the relics of noble looks. The fleshy nose, the pendulous cheek, the drooping mouth, had once been cast in looks of manly beauty. Heavy eyebrows above and heavy bags beneath spoiled the effect of a choleric blue eye, which age had not dimmed. The man was gross and yet haggard; it was not the padding of good living which clothed his bones, but a heaviness as of some dropsical malady. I could picture him in health a gaunt loose-limbed being, high-featured and swift and eager. He was dressed wholly in black velvet, with fresh ruffles and wristbands, and he wore heeled shoes with antique silver buckles. It was a figure of an older age which rose to greet me, in one hand a snuff-box and a purple handkerchief, and in the other a book with finger marking place. He made me a great bow as Madame uttered my name, and held out a hand with a kindly smile.

"Mr. Hervey-Townshend," he said, "we will speak English, if you please. I am fain to hear it again, for 'tis a tongue I love. I make you welcome, sir, for your own sake and for the sake of your kin. How is her honourable ladyship, your aunt? A week ago she sent me a letter."

I answered that she did famously, and wondered what cause of correspondence my worthy aunt could have with wandering nobles of Italy.

He motioned me to a chair between Madame and himself, while a servant set a candle on a shelf behind him. Then he proceeded to catechise me in excellent English, with now and then a phrase of French, as to the doings in my own land. Admirably informed this Italian gentleman proved himself. I defy you to find in Almack's more intelligent gossip. He inquired as to the chances of my Lord North and the mind of my Lord Rockingham. He had my Lord Shelburne's foibles at his fingers' ends. The habits of the Prince, the aims of the their ladyships of Dorset and Buckingham, the extravagance of this noble Duke and that right honourable gentleman were not hid from him. I answered discreetly yet frankly, for there was no ill-breeding in his curiosity. Rather it seemed like the inquiries of some fine lady, now buried deep in the country, as to the doings of a forsaken Mayfair. There was humour in it and something of pathos.

"My aunt must be a voluminous correspondent, sir," I said.

He laughed, "I have many friends in England who write to me, but I have seen none of them for long, and I doubt I may never see them again. Also in my youth I have been in England." And he sighed as at sorrowful recollection.

Then he showed the book in his hand. "See," he said, "here is one of your English writings, the greatest book I have ever happened on." It was a volume of Mr. Fielding. For a little he talked of books and poets. He admired Mr. Fielding profoundly, Dr. Smollet somewhat less, Mr. Richardson not at all. But he was clear that England had a monopoly of good writers, saving only my friend M. Rousseau, whom he valued, yet with reservations. Of the Italians he had no opinion. I instanced against him the plays of Signor Alfieri. He groaned, shook his head, and grew moody.

"Know you Scotland?" he asked suddenly.

I replied that I had visited Scotch cousins, but had no great estimation for the country. "It is too poor and jagged," I said, "for the taste of one who loves colour and sunshine and suave outlines." He sighed. "It is indeed a bleak land, but a kindly. When the sun shines at all he shines on the truest hearts in the world. I love its bleakness too. There is a spirit in the misty hills and the harsh sea-wind which inspires men to great deeds. Poverty and courage go often together, and my Scots, if they are poor, are as untamable as their mountains."

"You know the land, sir?" I asked.

"I have seen it, and I have known many Scots. You will find them in Paris and Avignon and Rome, with never a plack in their pockets. I have a feeling for exiles, sir, and I have pitied these poor people. They gave their all for the cause they followed."

Clearly the Count shared my aunt's views of history--those views which have made such sport for us often at Carteron. Stalwart Whig as I am, there was something in the tone of the old gentleman which made me feel a certain majesty in the lost cause.

"I am Whig in blood and Whig in principle," I said,--"but I have never denied that those Scots who followed the Chevalier were too good to waste on so trumpery a leader."

I had no sooner spoken the words than I felt that somehow I had been guilty of a betise.

"It may be so," said the Count. "I did not bid you here, sir, to argue on politics, on which I am assured we should differ. But I will ask you one question. The King of England is a stout upholder of the right of kings. How does he face the defection of his American possessions?"

"The nation takes it well enough, and as for his Majesty's feelings, there is small inclination to inquire into them. I conceive of the whole war as a blunder out of which we have come as we deserved. The day is gone by for the assertion of monarchic rights against the will of a people."

"May be. But take note that the King of England is suffering to-day as--how do you call him?--the Chevalier suffered forty years ago. 'The wheel has come full circle,' as your Shakespeare says. Time has wrought his revenge."

He was staring into a fire, which burned small and smokily.

"You think the day for kings is ended. I read it differently. The world will ever have need of kings. If a nation cast out one it will have to find another. And mark you, those later kings, created by the people, will bear a harsher hand than the old race who ruled as of right. Some day the world will regret having destroyed the kindly and legitimate line of monarchs and put in their place tyrants who govern by the sword or by flattering an idle mob.

This belated dogma would at other times have set me laughing, but the strange figure before me gave no impulse to merriment. I glanced at Madame, and saw her face grave and perplexed, and I thought I read a warning gleam in her eye. There was a mystery about the party which irritated me, but good breeding forbade me to seek a clue.

"You will permit me to retire, sir," I said. "I have but this morning come down from a long march among the mountains east of this valley. Sleeping in wayside huts and tramping those sultry paths make a man think pleasantly of bed."

The Count seemed to brighten at my words. "You are a marcher, sir, and love the mountains! Once I would gladly have joined you, for in my youth I was a great walker in hilly places. Tell me, now, how many miles will you cover in a day?"

I told him thirty at a stretch.

"Ah," he said, "I have done fifty, without food, over the roughest and mossiest mountains. I lived on what I shot, and for drink I had springwater. Nay, I am forgetting. There was another beverage, which I wager you have never tasted. Heard you ever, sir, of that eau de vie which the Scots call usquebagh? It will comfort a traveller as no thin Italian wine will comfort him. By my soul, you shall taste it. Charlotte, my dear, bid Oliphant fetch glasses and hot water and lemons. I will give Mr. Hervey-Townshend a sample of the brew. You English are all tetes-de-fer, sir, and are worthy of it."

The old man's face had lighted up, and for the moment his air had the jollity of youth. I would have accepted the entertainment had I not again caught Madame's eye. It said, unmistakably and with serious pleading, "Decline." I therefore made my excuses, urged fatigue, drowsiness, and a delicate stomach, bade my host good-night, and in deep mystification left the room.

Enlightenment came upon me as the door closed. There in the threshold stood the manservant whom they called Oliphant, erect as a sentry on guard. The sight reminded me of what I had once seen at Basle when by chance a Rhenish Grand Duke had shared the inn with me. Of a sudden a dozen clues linked together--the crowned notepaper, Scotland, my aunt Hervey's politics, the tale of old wanderings.

"Tell me," I said in a whisper, "who is the Count d'Albani, your master?" and I whistled softly a bar of "Charlie is my darling."

"Ay," said the man, without relaxing a muscle of his grim face. "It is the King of England--my king and yours."

II

In the small hours of the next morning I was awoke by a most unearthly sound. It was as if all the cats on all the roofs of Santa Chiara were sharpening their claws and wailing their battle-cries. Presently out of the noise came a kind of music--very slow, solemn, and melancholy. The notes ran up in great flights of ecstasy, and sunk anon to the tragic deeps. In spite of my sleepiness I was held spellbound and the musician had concluded with certain barbaric grunts before I had the curiosity to rise. It came from somewhere in the gallery of the inn, and as I stuck my head out of my door I had a glimpse of Oliphant, nightcap on head and a great bagpipe below his arm, stalking down the corridor.

The incident, for all the gravity of the music, seemed to give a touch of farce to my interview of the past evening. I had gone to bed with my mind full of sad stories of the deaths of kings. Magnificence in tatters has always affected my pity more deeply than tatters with no such antecedent, and a monarch out at elbows stood for me as the last irony of our mortal life. Here was a king whose misfortunes could find no parallel. He had been in his youth the hero of a high adventure, and his middle age had been spent in fleeting among the courts of Europe, and waiting as pensioner on the whims of his foolish but regnant brethren. I had heard tales of a growing sottishness, a decline in spirit, a squalid taste in pleasures. Small blame, I had always thought, to so ill-fated a princeling. And now I had chanced upon the gentleman in his dotage, travelling with a barren effort at mystery, attended by a sad-faced daughter and two ancient domestics. It was a lesson in the vanity of human wishes which the shallowest moralist would have noted. Nay, I felt more than the moral. Something human and kindly in the old fellow had caught my fancy. The decadence was too tragic to prose about, the decadent too human to moralise on. I had left the chamber of the--shall I say de jure King of England?--a sentimental adherent of the cause. But this business of the bagpipes touched the comic. To harry an old valet out of bed and set him droning on pipes in the small hours smacked of a theatrical taste, or at least of an undignified fancy. Kings in exile, if they wish to keep the tragic air, should not indulge in such fantastic serenades.

My mind changed again when after breakfast I fell in with Madame on the stair. She drew aside to let me pass, and then made as if she would speak to me. I gave her good-morning, and, my mind being full of her story, addressed her as "Excellency."

"I see, sir," she said, " hat you know the truth. I have to ask your forbearance for the concealment I practised yesterday. It was a poor requital for your generosity, but is it one of the shifts of our sad fortune. An uncrowned king must go in disguise or risk the laughter of every stable-boy. Besides, we are too poor to travel in state, even if we desired it."

Honestly, I knew not what to say. I was not asked to sympathise, having already revealed my politics, and yet the case cried out for sympathy. You remember, my dear aunt, the good Lady Culham, who was our Dorsetshire neighbour, and tried hard to mend my ways at Carteron? This poor Duchess--for so she called herself--was just such another. A woman made for comfort, housewifery, and motherhood, and by no means for racing about Europe in charge of a disreputable parent. I could picture her settled equably on a garden seat with a lapdog and needlework, blinking happily over green lawns and mildly rating an errant gardener. I could fancy her sitting in a summer parlour, very orderly and dainty, writing lengthy epistles to a tribe of nieces. I could see her marshalling a household in the family pew, or riding serenely in the family coach behind fat bay horses. But here, on an inn staircase, with a false name and a sad air of mystery, she was woefully out of place. I noted little wrinkles forming in the corners of her eyes, and the ravages of care beginning in the plump rosiness of her face. Be sure there was nothing appealing in her mien. She spoke with the air of a great lady, to whom the world is matter only for an afterthought. It was the facts that appealed and grew poignant from her courage.

"There is another claim upon your good nature," she said. "Doubtless you were awoke last night by Oliphant's playing upon the pipes. I rebuked the landlord for his insolence in protesting, but to you, a gentleman and a friend, an explanation is due. My father sleeps ill, and your conversation seems to have cast him into a train of sad memories. It has been his habit on such occasions to have the pipes played to him, since they remind him of friends and happier days. It is a small privilege for an old man, and he does not claim it often."

I declared that the music had only pleased, and that I would welcome its repetition. Where upon she left me with a little bow and an invitation to join them that day at dinner, while I departed into the town on my own errands. I returned before midday, and was seated at an arbour in the garden, busy with letters, when there hove in sight the gaunt figure of Oliphant. He hovered around me, if such a figure can be said to hover, with the obvious intention of addressing me. The fellow had caught my fancy, and I was willing to see more of him. His face might have been hacked out of grey granite, his clothes hung loosely on his spare bones, and his stockined shanks would have done no discredit to Don Quixote. There was no dignity in his air, only a steady and enduring sadness. Here, thought I, is the one of the establishment who most commonly meets the shock of the world's buffets. I called him by name and asked him his desires.

It appeared that he took me for a Jacobite, for he began a rigmarole about loyalty and hard fortune. I hastened to correct him, and he took the correction with the same patient despair with which he took all things. 'Twas but another of the blows of Fate.

"At any rate," he said in a broad Scotch accent, "ye come of kin that has helpit my maister afore this. I've many times heard tell o' Herveys and Townshends in England, and a' folk said they were on the richt side. Ye're maybe no a freend, but ye're a freend's freend, or I wadna be speirin' at ye."

I was amused at the prologue, and waited on the tale. It soon came. Oliphant, it appeared, was the purse-bearer of the household, and woeful straits that poor purse-bearer must have been often put to. I questioned him as to his master's revenues, but could get no clear answer. There were payments due next month in Florence which would solve the difficulties for the winter, but in the meantime expenditure had beaten income. Travelling had cost much, and the Count must have his small comforts. The result in plain words was that Oliphant had not the wherewithal to frank the company to Florence; indeed, I doubted if he could have paid the reckoning in Santa Chiara. A loan was therefore sought from a friend's friend, meaning myself.

I was very really embarrassed. Not that I would not have given willingly, for I had ample resources at the moment and was mightily concerned about the sad household. But I knew that the little Duchess would take Oliphant's ears from his head if she guessed that he had dared to borrow from me, and that, if I lent, her back would for ever be turned against me. And yet, what would follow on my refusal? In a day of two there would be a pitiful scene with mine host, and as like as not some of their baggage detained as security for payment. I did not love the task of conspiring behind the lady's back, but if it could be contrived 'twas indubitably the kindest course. I glared sternly at Oliphant, who met me with his pathetic, dog-like eyes.

"You know that your mistress would never consent to the request you have made of me?"

"I ken," he said humbly. "But payin' is my job, and I simply havena the siller. It's no the first time it has happened, and it's a sair trial for them both to be flung out o' doors by a foreign hostler because they canna meet his charges. But, sir, if ye can lend to me, ye may be certain that her leddyship will never, hear a word o't. Puir thing, she takes nae thocht o' where the siller comes frae, ony mair than the lilies o' the field."

I became a conspirator. "You swear, Oliphant, by all you hold sacred, to breathe nothing of this to your mistress, and if she should suspect, to lie like a Privy Councillor?"

A flicker of a smile crossed his face. "I'll lee like a Scotch packman, and the Father o' lees could do nae mair. You need have no fear for your siller, sir. I've aye repaid when I borrowed, though you may have to wait a bittock." And the strange fellow strolled off.

At dinner no Duchess appeared till long after the appointed hour, nor was there any sign of Oliphant. When she came at last with Cristine, her eyes looked as if she had been crying, and she greeted me with remote courtesy. My first thought was that Oliphant had revealed the matter of the loan, but presently I found that the lady's trouble was far different. Her father, it seemed, was ill again with his old complaint. What that was I did not ask, nor did the Duchess reveal it.

We spoke in French, for I had discovered that this was her favourite speech. There was no Oliphant to wait on us, and the inn servants were always about, so it was well to have a tongue they did not comprehend. The lady was distracted and sad. When I inquired feelingly as to the general condition of her father's health she parried the question, and when I offered my services she disregarded my words. It was in truth a doleful meal, while the faded Cristine sat like a sphinx staring into vacancy. I spoke of England and of her friends, of Paris and Versailles, of Avignon where she had spent some years, and of the amenities of Florence, which she considered her home. But it was like talking to a nunnery door. I got nothing but "It is indeed true, sir," or "Do you say so, sir!" till my energy began to sink. Madame perceived my discomfort, and, as she rose, murmured an apology. "Pray forgive my distraction, but I am poor company when my father is ill. I have a foolish mind, easily frightened. Nay, nay!" she went on when I again offered help, "the illness is trifling. It will pass off by to-morrow, or at the latest the next day. Only I had looked forward to some ease at Santa Chiara, and the promise is belied."

As it chanced that evening, returning to the inn, I passed by the north side where the windows of the Count's room looked over a little flower-garden abutting on the courtyard. The dusk was falling, and a lamp had been lit which gave a glimpse into the interior. The sick man was standing by the window, his figure flung into relief by the lamplight. If he was sick, his sickness was of a curious type. His face was ruddy, his eye wild, and, his wig being off, his scanty hair stood up oddly round his head. He seemed to be singing, but I could not catch the sound through the shut casement. Another figure in the room, probably Oliphant, laid a hand on the Count's shoulder, drew him from the window, and closed the shutter.

It needed only the recollection of stories which were the property of all Europe to reach a conclusion on the gentleman's illness. The legitimate King of England was very drunk.

As I went to my room that night I passed the Count's door. There stood Oliphant as sentry, more grim and haggard than ever, and I thought that his eye met mine with a certain intelligence. From inside the room came a great racket. There was the sound of glasses falling, then a string of oaths, English, French, and for all I know, Irish, rapped out in a loud drunken voice. A pause, and then came the sound of maudlin singing. It pursued me along the gallery, an old childish song, delivered as if 'twere a pot-house catch-

"Qu'est-ce qui passe ici si tard, Compagnons de la Marjolaine---"

One of the late-going company of the Marjolaine hastened to bed. This king in exile, with his melancholy daughter, was becoming too much for him.

III

It was just before noon next day that the travellers arrived. I was sitting in the shady loggia of the inn, reading a volume of De Thou, when there drove up to the door two coaches. Out of the first descended very slowly and stiffly four gentlemen; out of the second four servants and a quantity of baggage. As it chanced there was no one about, the courtyard slept its sunny noontide sleep, and the only movement was a lizard on the wall and a buzz of flies by the fountain. Seeing no sign of the landlord, one of the travellers approached me with a grave inclination.

"This is the inn called the Tre Croci, sir?" he asked.

I said it was, and shouted on my own account for the host. Presently that personage arrived with a red face and a short wind, having ascended rapidly from his own cellar. He was awed by the dignity of the travellers, and made none of his usual protests of incapacity. The servants filed off solemnly with the baggage, and the four gentlemen set themselves down beside me in the loggia and ordered each a modest flask of wine.

At first I took them for our countrymen, but as I watched them the conviction vanished. All four were tall and lean beyond the average of mankind. They wore suits of black, with antique starched frills to their shirts; their hair was their own and unpowdered. Massive buckles of an ancient pattern adorned their square-toed shoes, and the canes they carried were like the yards of a small vessel. They were four merchants, I had guessed, of Scotland, maybe, or of Newcastle, but their voices were not Scotch, and their air had no touch of commerce. Take the heavy-browed preoccupation of a Secretary of State, add the dignity of a bishop, the sunburn of a fox-hunter, and something of the disciplined erectness of a soldier, and you may perceive the manner of these four gentlemen. By the side of them my assurance vanished. Compared with their Olympian serenity my Person seemed fussy and servile. Even so, I mused, must Mr. Franklin have looked when baited in Parliament by the Tory pack. The reflection gave me the cue. Presently I caught from their conversation the word "Washington," and the truth flashed upon me. I was in the presence of four of Mr. Franklin's countrymen. Having never seen an American in the flesh, I rejoiced at the chance of enlarging my acquaintance.

They brought me into the circle by a polite question as to the length of road to Verona. Soon introductions followed. My name intrigued them, and they were eager to learn of my kinship to Uncle Charles. The eldest of the four, it appeared, was Mr. Galloway out of Maryland. Then came two brothers, Sylvester by name, of Pennsylvania, and last Mr. Fish, a lawyer of New York. All four had campaigned in the late war, and all four were members of the Convention, or whatever they call their rough-and-ready parliament. They were modest in their behaviour, much disinclined to speak of their past, as great men might be whose reputation was world-wide. Somehow the names stuck in my memory. I was certain that I had heard them linked with some stalwart fight or some moving civil deed or some defiant manifesto. The making of history was in their steadfast eye and the grave lines of the mouth. Our friendship flourished mightily in a brief hour, and brought me the invitation, willingly accepted, to sit with them at dinner.

There was no sign of the Duchess or Cristine or Oliphant. Whatever had happened, that household to-day required all hands on deck, and I was left alone with the Americans. In my day I have supped with the Macaronies, I have held up my head at the Cocoa Tree, I have avoided the floor at hunt dinners, I have drunk glass to glass with Tom Carteron. But never before have I seen such noble consumers of good liquor as those four gentlemen from beyond the Atlantic. They drank the strong red Cyprus as if it had been spring-water. "The dust of your Italian roads takes some cleansing, Mr. Townshend," was their only excuse, but in truth none was needed. The wine seemed only to thaw their iron decorum. Without any surcease of dignity they grew communicative, and passed from lands to peoples and from peoples to constitutions. Before we knew it we were embarked upon high politics.

Naturally we did not differ on the war. Like me, they held it to have been a grievous necessity. They had no bitterness against England, only regrets for her blunders. Of his Majesty they spoke with respect, of his Majesty's advisers with dignified condemnation. They thought highly of our troops in America; less highly of our generals.

"Look you, sir," said Mr. Galloway, "in a war such as we have witnessed the Almighty is the only strategist. You fight against the forces of Nature, and a newcomer little knows that the success or failure of every operation he can conceive depends not upon generalship, but upon the confirmation of a vast country. Our generals, with this in mind and with fewer men, could make all your schemes miscarry. Had the English soldiers not been of such stubborn stuff, we should have been victors from the first. Our leader was not General Washington but General America, and his brigadiers were forests, swamps, lakes, rivers, and high mountains."

"And now," I said, "having won, you have the greatest of human experiments before you. Your business is to show that the Saxon stock is adaptable to a republic."

It seemed to me that they exchanged glances.

"We are not pedants," said Mr. Fish, "and have no desire to dispute about the form of a constitution. A people may be as free under a king as under a senate. Liberty is not the lackey of any type of government."

These were strange words from a member of a race whom I had thought wedded to the republicanism of Helvidius Priscus.

"As a loyal subject of a monarchy," I said, "I must agree with you. But your hands are tied, for I cannot picture the establishment of a House of Washington and--if not, where are you to turn for your sovereign?"

Again a smile seemed to pass among the four.

"We are experimenters, as you say, sir, and must go slowly. In the meantime, we have an authority which keeps peace and property safe. We are at leisure to cast our eyes round and meditate on the future."

"Then, gentlemen," said I, "you take an excellent way of meditation in visiting this museum of old sovereignties. Here you have the relics of any government you please--a dozen republics, tyrannies, theocracies, merchant confederations, kingdoms, and more than one empire. You have your choice. I am tolerably familiar with the land, and if I can assist you I am at your service."

They thanked me gravely "We have letters," said Mr. Galloway; "one in especial is to a gentleman whom we hope to meet in this place. Have you heard in your travels of the Count of Albany?"

"He has arrived," said I, "two days ago. Even now he is in the chamber above us at dinner."

The news interested them hugely.

"You have seen him?" they cried. "What is he like?"

"An elderly gentleman in poor health, a man who has travelled much, and, I judge, has suffered something from fortune. He has a fondness for the English, so you will be welcome, sirs; but he was indisposed yesterday, and may still be unable to receive you. His daughter travels with him and tends his old age."

" And you--you have spoken with him?"

"The night before last I was in his company. We talked of many things, including the late war. He is somewhat of your opinion on matters of government."

The four looked at each other, and then Mr. Galloway rose.

"I ask your permission, Mr. Townshend, to consult for a moment with my friends. The matter is of some importance, and I would beg you to await us." So saying, he led the others out of doors, and I heard them withdraw to a corner of the loggia. Now, thought I, there is something afoot, and my long-sought romance approaches fruition. The company of the Marjolaine, whom the Count had sung of, have arrived at last.

Presently they returned and seated themselves at the table.

"You can be of great assistance to us, Mr. Townshend, and we would fain take you into our confidence. Are you aware who is this Count of Albany?"

I nodded. "It is a thin disguise to one familiar with history."

"Have you reached any estimate of his character or capabilities? You speak to friends, and, let me tell you, it is a matter which deeply concerns the Count's interests."

"I think him a kindly and pathetic old gentleman. He naturally bears the mark of forty years' sojourn in the wilderness."

Mr. Galloway took snuff.

"We have business with him, but it is business which stands in need of an agent. There is no one in the Count's suite with whom we could discuss affairs?"

"There is his daughter."

"Ah, but she would scarcely suit the case. Is there no man--a friend, and yet not a member of the family who can treat with us?"

I replied that I thought that I was the only being in Santa Chiara who answered the description.

"If you will accept the task, Mr. Townshend, you are amply qualified. We will be frank with you and reveal our business. We are on no less an errand than to offer the Count of Albany a crown.

I suppose I must have had some suspicion of their purpose, and yet the revelation of it fell on me like a thunderclap. I could only stare owlishly at my four grave gentlemen.

Mr. Galloway went on unperturbed. "I have told you that in America we are not yet republicans. There are those among us who favour a republic, but they are by no means a majority. We have got rid of a king who misgoverned us, but we have no wish to get rid of kingship. We want a king of our own choosing, and we would get with him all the ancient sanctions of monarchy. The Count of Albany is of the most illustrious royal stock in Europe--he is, if legitimacy goes for anything, the rightful King of Britain. Now, if the republican party among us is to be worsted, we must come before the nation with a powerful candidate for their favour. You perceive my drift? What more potent appeal to American pride than to say: 'We have got rid of King George; we choose of our own free will the older line and King Charles'?"

I said foolishly that I thought monarchy had had its day, and that 'twas idle to revive it.

"That is a sentiment well enough under a monarchical government; but we, with a clean page to write upon, do not share it. You know your ancient historians. Has not the repository of the chief power always been the rock on which republicanism has shipwrecked? If that power is given to the chief citizen, the way is prepared for the tyrant. If it abides peacefully in a royal house, it abides with cyphers who dignify, without obstructing, a popular constitution. Do not mistake me, Mr. Townshend. This is no whim of a sentimental girl, but the reasoned conclusion of the men who achieved our liberty. There is every reason to believe that General Washington shares our views, and Mr. Hamilton, whose name you may know, is the inspirer of our mission."

"But the Count is an old man," I urged; for I knew not where to begin in my exposition of the hopelessness of their errand.

"By so much the better. We do not wish a young king who may be fractious. An old man tempered by misfortune is what our purpose demands."

"He has also his failings. A man cannot lead his life for forty years and retain all the virtues."

At that one of the Sylvesters spoke sharply. "I have heard such gossip, but I do not credit it. I have not forgotten Preston and Derby."

I made my last objection. "He has no posterity--legitimate posterity--to carry on his line."

The four gentlemen smiled. "That happens to be his chiefest recommendation," said Mr. Galloway. "It enables us to take the House of Stuart on trial. We need a breathing-space and leisure to look around; but unless we establish the principle of monarchy at once the republicans will forestall us. Let us get our king at all costs, and during the remaining years of his life we shall have time to settle the succession problem.

"We have no wish to saddle ourselves for good with a race who might prove burdensome. If King Charles fails he has no son, and we can look elsewhere for a better monarch. You perceive the reason of my view?"

I did, and I also perceived the colossal absurdity of the whole business. But I could not convince them of it, for they met my objections with excellent arguments. Nothing save a sight of the Count would, I feared, disillusion them.

"You wish me to make this proposal on your behalf?" I asked.

"We shall make the proposal ourselves, but we desire you to prepare the way for us. He is an elderly man, and should first be informed of our purpose."

"There is one person whom I beg leave to consult--the Duchess, his daughter. It may be that the present is an ill moment for approaching the Count, and the affair requires her sanction."

They agreed, and with a very perplexed mind I went forth to seek the lady. The irony of the thing was too cruel, and my heart ached for her. In the gallery I found Oliphant packing some very shabby trunks, and when I questioned him he told me that the family were to leave Santa Chiara on the morrow. Perchance the Duchess had awakened to the true state of their exchequer, or perchance she thought it well to get her father on the road again as a cure for his ailment.

I discovered Cristine, and begged for an interview with her mistress on an urgent matter. She led me to the Duchess's room, and there the evidence of poverty greeted me openly. All the little luxuries of the menage had gone to the Count. The poor lady's room was no better than a servant's garret, and the lady herself sat stitching a rent in a travelling cloak. She rose to greet me with alarm in her eyes.

As briefly as I could I set out the facts of my amazing mission. At first she seemed scarcely to hear me. "What do they want with him?" she asked. "He can give them nothing. He is no friend to the Americans or to any people who have deposed their sovereign." Then, as she grasped my meaning, her face flushed.

"It is a heartless trick, Mr. Townshend. I would fain think you no party to it."

"Believe me, dear madame, it is no trick. The men below are in sober earnest. You have but to see their faces to know that theirs is no wild adventure. I believe sincerely that they have the power to implement their promise."

"But it is madness. He is old and worn and sick. His day is long past for winning a crown."

"All this I have said, but it does not move them." And I told her rapidly Mr. Galloway's argument. She fell into a muse. "At the eleventh hour! Nay, too late, too late. Had he been twenty years younger, what a stroke of fortune! Fate bears too hard on us, too hard!"

Then she turned to me fiercely. "You have no doubt heard, sir, the gossip about my father, which is on the lips of every fool in Europe. Let us have done with this pitiful make-believe. My father is a sot. Nay, I do not blame him. I blame his enemies and his miserable destiny. But there is the fact. Were he not old, he would still be unfit to grasp a crown and rule over a turbulent people. He flees from one city to another, but he cannot flee from himself. That is his illness on which you condoled with me yesterday."

The lady's control was at breaking-point. Another moment and I expected a torrent of tears. But they did not come. With a great effort she regained her composure.

"Well, the gentlemen must have an answer. You will tell them that the Count, my father--nay--give him his true title if you care--is vastly obliged to them for the honour they have done him, but would decline on account of his age and infirmities. You know how to phrase a decent refusal."

"Pardon me," said I, "but I might give them that answer till doomsday and never content them. They have not travelled many thousand miles to be put off by hearsay evidence. Nothing will satisfy them but an interview with your father himself.

"It is impossible," she said sharply.

"Then we must expect the renewed attentions of our American friends. They will wait till they see him."

She rose and paced the room.

"They must go," she repeated many times. "If they see him sober he will accept with joy, and we shall be the laughing-stock of the world. I tell you it cannot be. I alone know how immense is the impossibility. He cannot afford to lose the last rags of his dignity, the last dregs of his ease. They must not see him. I will speak with them myself."

"They will be honoured, madame, but I do not think they will be convinced. They are what we call in my land 'men of business.' They will not be content till they get the Count's reply from his own lips."

A new Duchess seemed to have arisen, a woman of quick action and sharp words.

"So be it. They shall see him. Oh, I am sick to death of fine sentiments and high loyalty and all the vapouring stuff I have lived among for years. All I ask for myself and my father is a little peace, and, by Heaven! I shall secure it. If nothing will kill your gentlemen's folly but truth, why, truth they shall have. They shall see my father, and this very minute. Bring them up, Mr. Townshend, and usher them into the presence of the rightful King of England. You will find him alone." She stopped her walk and looked out of the window.

I went back in a hurry to the Americans. "I am bidden to bring you to the Count's chamber. He is alone and will see you. These are the commands of madame his daughter."

"Good!" said Mr. Galloway, and all four, grave gentlemen as they were, seemed to brace themselves to a special dignity as befitted ambassadors to a king. I led them upstairs, tapped at the Count's door, and, getting no answer, opened it and admitted them.

And this was what we saw. The furniture was in disorder, and on a couch lay an old man sleeping a heavy drunken sleep. His mouth was open and his breath came stertorously. The face was purple, and large purple veins stood out on the mottled forehead. His scanty white hair was draggled over his cheek. On the floor was a broken glass, wet stains still lay on the boards, and the place reeked of spirits. The four looked for a second--I do not think longer at him whom they would have made their king. They did not look at each other. With one accord they moved out, and Mr. Fish, who was last, closed the door very gently behind him.

In the hall below Mr. Galloway turned to me. "Our mission is ended, Mr. Townshend. I have to thank you for your courtesy." Then to the others, "If we order the coaches now, we may get well on the way to Verona ere sundown."

An hour later two coaches rolled out of the courtyard of the Tre Croci. As they passed, a window was half-opened on the upper floor, and a head looked out. A line of a song came down, a song sung in a strange quavering voice. It was the catch I had heard the night before:

"Qu'est-ce qui passe ici si tard, Compagnons de la Marjolaine--e!"

It was true. The company came late indeed--too late by forty years. . . .

AVIGNON
1759

Hearts to break but nane to sell, Gear to tine but nane to hain;-- We maun dree a weary spell Ere our lad comes back again.

I walk abroad on winter days, When storms have stripped the wide champaign, For northern winds have norland ways, And scents of Badenoch haunt the rain. And by the lipping river path, When in the fog the Rhone runs grey, I see the heather of the Strath, And watch the salmon leap in Spey.

The hills are feathered with young trees, I set them for my children's boys. I made a garden deep in ease, A pleasance for my lady's joys. Strangers have heired them. Long ago She died,--kind fortune thus to die; And my one son by Beauly flow Gave up the soul that could not lie.

Old, elbow-worn, and pinched I bide The final toll the gods may take. The laggard years have quenched my pride; They cannot kill the ache, the ache.

Weep not the dead, for they have sleep Who lie at home: but ah, for me In the deep grave my heart will weep With longing for my lost countrie.

Hearts to break but nane to sell, Gear to tine but nane to hain;-- We maun dree a weary spell Ere our lad comes back again.

II

A LUCID INTERVAL

To adopt the opening words of a more famous tale, "The truth of this strange matter is what the world has long been looking for." The events which I propose to chronicle were known to perhaps a hundred people in London whose fate brings them into contact with politics. The consequences were apparent to all the world, and for one hectic fortnight tinged the soberest newspapers with saffron, drove more than one worthy election agent to an asylum, and sent whole batches of legislators to Continental cures. "But no reasonable explanation of the mystery has been forthcoming until now, when a series of chances gave the key into my hands.

Lady Caerlaverock is my aunt, and I was present at the two remarkable dinner-parties which form the main events in this tale. I was also taken into her confidence during the terrible fortnight which intervened between them. Like everybody else, I was hopelessly in the dark, and could only accept what happened as a divine interposition. My first clue came when James, the Caerlaverocks' second footman, entered my service as valet, and being a cheerful youth chose to gossip while he shaved me. I checked him, but he babbled on, and I could not choose but learn something about the disposition of the Caerlaverock household below stairs. I learned--what I knew before--that his lordship had an inordinate love for curries, a taste acquired during some troubled years as Indian Viceroy. I had often eaten that admirable dish at his table, and had heard him boast of the skill of the Indian cook who prepared it. James, it appeared, did not hold with the Orient in the kitchen. He described the said Indian gentleman as a "nigger," and expressed profound distrust of his ways. He referred darkly to the events of the year before, which in some distorted way had reached the servants' ears. "We always thought as 'ow it was them niggers as done it," he declared; and when I questioned him on his use of the plural, admitted that at the time in question "there 'ad been more nor one nigger 'anging about the kitchen."

Pondering on these sayings, I asked myself if it were not possible that the behaviour of certain eminent statesmen was due to some strange devilry of the East, and I made a vow to abstain in future from the Caerlaverock curries. But last month my brother returned from India, and I got the whole truth. He was staying with me in Scotland, and in the smoking-room the talk turned on occultism in the East. I declared myself a sceptic, and George was stirred. He asked me rudely what I knew about it, and proceeded to make a startling confession of faith. He was cross-examined by the others, and retorted with some of his experiences. Finding an incredulous audience, his tales became more defiant, until he capped them all with one monstrous yarn. He maintained that in a Hindu family of his acquaintance there had been transmitted the secret of a drug, capable of altering a man's whole temperament until the antidote was administered. It would turn a coward into a bravo, a miser into a spendthrift, a rake into a fakir. Then, having delivered his manifesto he got up abruptly and went to bed.

I followed him to his room, for something in the story had revived a memory. By dint of much persuasion I dragged from the somnolent George various details. The family in question were Beharis, large landholders dwelling near the Nepal border. He had known old Ram Singh for years, and had seen him twice since his return from England. He got the story from him under no promise of secrecy, for the family drug was as well known in the neighbourhood as the nine incarnations of Krishna. He had no doubt about the truth of it, for he had positive proof. "And others besides me," said George. "Do you remember when

Vennard had a lucid interval a couple of years ago and talked sense for once? That was old Ram Singh's doing, for he told me about it."

Three years ago it seems the Government of India saw fit to appoint a commission to inquire into land tenure on the Nepal border. Some of the feudal Rajahs had been "birsing yont," like the Breadalbanes, and the smaller zemindars were gravely disquieted. The result of the commission was that Ram Singh had his boundaries rectified, and lost a mile or two of country which his hard-fisted fathers had won.

I know nothing of the rights of the matter, but there can be no doubt about Ram Singh's dissatisfaction. He appealed to the law courts, but failed to upset the commission's finding, and the Privy Council upheld the Indian judgment. Thereupon in a flowery and eloquent document he laid his case before the Viceroy, and was told that the matter was closed. Now Ram Singh came of a fighting stock, so he straightway took ship to England to petition the Crown. He petitioned Parliament, but his petition went into the bag behind the Speaker's chair, from which there is no return. He petitioned the King, but was courteously informed that he must approach the Department concerned. He tried the Secretary of State for India, and had an interview with Abinger Vennard, who was very rude to him, and succeeded in mortally insulting the feudal aristocrat. He appealed to the Prime Minister, and was warned off by a harassed private secretary. The handful of members of Parliament who make Indian grievances their stock-in-trade fought shy of him, for indeed Ram Singh's case had no sort of platform appeal in it, and his arguments were flagrantly undemocratic. But they sent him to Lord Caerlaverock, for the ex-viceroy loved to be treated as a kind of consul-general for India. But this Protector of the Poor proved a broken reed. He told Ram Singh flatly that he was a belated feudalist, which was true; and implied that he was a land-grabber, which was not true, Ram Singh having only enjoyed the fruits of his fore-bears' enterprise. Deeply incensed, the appellant shook the dust of Caerlaverock House from his feet, and sat down to plan a revenge upon the Government which had wronged him. And in his wrath he thought of the heirloom of his house, the drug which could change men's souls.

It happened that Lord Caerlaverock cook's came from the same neighbourhood as Ram Singh. This cook, Lal Muhammad by name, was one of a large poor family, hangers-on of Ram Singh's house. The aggrieved landowner summoned him, and demanded as of right his humble services. Lal Muhammad, who found his berth to his liking, hesitated, quibbled, but was finally overborne. He suggested a fee for his services, but hastily withdrew when Ram Singh sketched a few of the steps he proposed to take on his return by way of punishing Lal Muhammad's insolence on Lal Muhammad's household. Then he got to business. There was a great dinner next week--so he had learned from Jephson, the butler--and more than one member of the Government would honour Caerlaverock House by his presence. With deference he suggested this as a fitting occasion for the experiment, and Ram Singh was pleased to assent.

I can picture these two holding their meetings in the South Kensington lodgings where Ram Singh dwelt. We know from James, the second footman, that they met also at Caerlaverock House, no doubt that Ram Singh might make certain that his orders were duly obeyed. I can see the little packet of clear grains--I picture them like small granulated sugar--added to the condiments, and soon dissolved out of sight. The deed was done; the cook returned to Bloomsbury and Ram Singh to Gloucester Road, to await with the patient certainty of the East the consummation of a great vengeance.

II

My wife was at Kissengen, and I was dining with the Caerlaverocks en garcon. When I have not to wait upon the adornment of the female person I am a man of punctual habits, and I reached the house as the hall clock chimed the quarter-past. My poor friend, Tommy Deloraine, arrived along with me, and we ascended the staircase together. I call him "my poor friend," for at the moment Tommy was under the weather. He had the misfortune to be a marquis, and a very rich one, and at the same time to be in love with Claudia Barriton. Neither circumstance was in itself an evil, but the combination made for tragedy. For Tommy's twenty-five years of healthy manhood, his cleanly-made up-standing figure, his fresh countenance and cheerful laugh, were of no avail in the lady's eyes when set against the fact that he was an idle peer. Miss Claudia was a charming girl, with a notable bee in her bonnet. She was burdened with the cares of the State, and had no patience with any one who took them lightly. To her mind the social fabric was rotten beyond repair, and her purpose was frankly destructive. I remember some of her phrases: "A bold and generous policy of social amelioration"; "The development of a civic conscience"; "A strong hand to lop off decaying branches from the trunk of the State." I have no fault to find with her creed, but I objected to its practical working when it took the shape of an inhuman hostility to that devout lover, Tommy Deloraine. She had refused him, I believe, three times, with every circumstance of scorn. The first time she had analysed his character, and described him as a bundle of attractive weaknesses. "The only forces I recognise are those of intellect and conscience," she had said, "and you have neither." The second time--it was after he had been to Canada on the staff--she spoke of the irreconcilability of their political ideals. "You are an Imperialist," she said, "and believe in an empire of conquest for the benefit of the few. I want a little island with a rich life for all." Tommy declared that he would become a Doukhobor to please her, but she said something about the inability of Ethiopians to change their skin. The third time she hinted vaguely that there was "another." The star of Abinger Vennard was now blazing in the firmament, and she had conceived a platonic admiration for him. The truth is that Miss Claudia, with all her cleverness, was very young and--dare I say it? --rather silly.

Caerlaverock was stroking his beard, his legs astraddle on the hearthrug, with something appallingly viceregal in his air, when Mr. and Mrs. Alexander Cargill were announced. The Home Secretary was a joy to behold. He had the face of an elderly and pious bookmaker, and a voice in which lurked the indescribable Scotch quality of "unction." When he was talking you had only to shut your eyes to imagine yourself in some lowland kirk on a hot Sabbath morning. He had been a distinguished advocate before he left the law for politics, and had swayed juries of his countrymen at his will. The man was extraordinarily efficient on a platform. There were unplumbed depths of emotion in his eye, a juicy sentiment in his voice, an overpowering tenderness in his manner, which gave to politics the glamour of a revival meeting. He wallowed in obvious pathos, and his hearers, often unwillingly, wallowed with him. I have never listened to any orator at once so offensive and so horribly effective. There was no appeal too base for him, and none too august: by some subtle alchemy he blended the arts of the prophet and the fishwife. He had discovered a new kind of language. Instead of "the hungry millions," or "the toilers," or any of the numerous synonyms for our masters, he invented the phrase, "Goad's people." "I shall never rest," so ran his great declaration, "till Goad's green fields and Goad's clear waters are free to Goad's people." I remember how on this occasion he pressed my hand with his famous cordiality, looked gravely and earnestly into my face, and then gazed sternly into vacancy. It was a fine picture of genius descending for a moment from its hill-top to show how close it was to poor humanity.

Then came Lord Mulross, a respectable troglodytic peer, who represented the one sluggish element in a swiftly progressing Government. He was an oldish man with bushy whiskers and a reputed mastery of the French tongue. A Whig, who had never changed his creed one iota, he was highly valued by the country as a sober element in the nation's councils, and endured by the Cabinet as necessary ballast. He did not conceal his dislike for certain of his colleagues, notably Mr. Vennard and Mr. Cargill.

When Miss Barriton arrived with her stepmother the party was almost complete. She entered with an air of apologising for her prettiness. Her manner with old men was delightful, and I watched with interest the unbending of Caerlaverock and the simplifying of Mr. Cargill in her presence. Deloraine, who was talking feverishly to Mrs. Cargill, started as if to go and greet her, thought better of it, and continued his conversation. The lady swept the room with her eye, but did not acknowledge his presence. She floated off with Mr. Cargill to a window-corner, and metaphorically sat at his feet. I saw Deloraine saying things behind his moustache, while he listened to Mrs. Cargill's new cure for dyspepsia.

Last of all, twenty minutes late, came Abinger Vennard. He made a fine stage entrance, walking swiftly with a lowering brow to his hostess, and then glaring fiercely round the room as if to challenge criticism. I have heard Deloraine, in a moment of irritation, describe him as a "Pre-Raphaelite attorney," but there could be no denying his good looks. He had a bad, loose figure, and a quantity of studiously neglected hair, but his face was the face of a young Greek. A certain kind of political success gives a man the manners of an actor, and both Vennard and Cargill bristled with self-consciousness. You could see it in the way they patted their hair, squared their shoulders, and shifted their feet to positions loved by sculptors.

"Well, Vennard, what's the news from the House?" Caerlaverock asked.

"Simpson is talking," said Vennard wearily. "He attacks me, of course. He says he has lived forty years in India--as if that mattered! When will people recognise that the truths of democratic policy are independent of time and space? Liberalism is a category, an eternal mode of thought, which cannot be overthrown by any trivial happenings. I am sick of the word 'facts.' I long for truths."

Miss Barriton's eyes brightened, and Cargill said, "Excellent." Lord Mulross, who was a little deaf, and in any case did not understand the language, said loudly to my aunt that he wished there was a close time for legislation.

"The open season for grouse should be the close season for politicians."

And then we went down to dinner.

Miss Barriton sat on my left hand, between Deloraine and me, and it was clear she was discontented with her position. Her eyes wandered down the table to Vennard, who had taken in an American duchess, and seemed to be amused at her prattle. She looked with disfavour at Deloraine, and turned to me as the lesser of two evils.

I was tactless enough to say that I thought there was a good deal in Lord Mulross's view. "Oh, how can you?" she cried. "Is there a close season for the wants of the people? It sounds to me perfectly horrible the way you talk of government, as if it were a game for idle men of the upper classes. I want professional politicians, men who give their whole heart and soul to the service of the State. I know the kind of member you and Lord Deloraine like--a rich young man who eats and drinks too much, and thinks the real business of life is killing little birds. He travels abroad and shoots some big game, and then comes home and vapours about the Empire. He knows nothing about realities, and will go down before the men who take the world seriously."

I am afraid I laughed, but Deloraine, who had been listening, was in no mood to be amused.

"I don't think you are quite fair to us, Miss Claudia," he said slowly. "We take things seriously enough, the things we know about. We can't be expected to know about everything, and the misfortune is that the things I care about don't interest you. But they are important enough for all that."

"Hush," said the lady rudely. "I want to hear what Mr. Vennard is saying."

Mr. Vennard was addressing the dinner-table as if it were a large public meeting. It was a habit he had, for he had no mind to confine the pearls of his wisdom to his immediate neighbours. His words were directed to Caerlaverock at the far end.

"In my opinion this craze for the scientific stand-point is not merely overdone--it is radically vicious. Human destinies cannot be treated as if they were inert objects under the microscope. The cold-blooded logical way of treating a problem is in almost every case the wrong way. Heart and imagination to me are more vital than intellect. I have the courage to be illogical, to defy facts for the sake of an ideal, in the certainty that in time facts will fall into conformity. My Creed may be put in the words of Newman's favourite quotation: Non in dialectica complacuit Deo salvum facere populum suum--Not in cold logic is it God's will that His people should find salvation."

"It is profoundly true," sighed Mr. Cargill, and Miss Claudia's beaming eyes proved her assent. The moment of destiny, though I did not know it, had arrived. The entree course had begun, and of the two entrees one was the famous Caerlaverock curry. Now on a hot July evening in London there are more attractive foods than curry seven times heated, MORE INDICO. I doubt if any guest would have touched it, had not our host in his viceregal voice called the attention of the three ministers to its merits, while explaining that under doctor's orders he was compelled to refrain for a season. The result was that Mulross, Cargill, and Vennard alone of the men partook of it. Miss Claudia, alone of the women, followed suit in the fervour of her hero-worship. She ate a mouthful, and then drank rapidly two glasses of water.

My narrative of the events which followed is based rather on what I should have seen than on what I saw. I had not the key, and missed much which otherwise would have been plain to me. For example, if I had known the secret, I must have seen Miss Claudia's gaze cease to rest upon Vennard and the adoration die out of her eyes. I must have noticed her face soften to the unhappy Deloraine. As it was, I did not remark her behaviour, till I heard her say to her neighbour--

"Can't you get hold of Mr. Vennard and forcibly cut his hair?"

Deloraine looked round with a start. Miss Barriton's tone was intimate and her face friendly.

"Some people think it picturesque," he said in serious bewilderment.

"Oh, yes, picturesque--like a hair-dresser's young man!" she shrugged her shoulders. He looks as if he had never been out of doors in his life."

Now, whatever the faults of Tommy's appearance, he had a wholesome sunburnt face, and he knew it. This speech of Miss Barriton's cheered him enormously, for he argued that if she had fallen out of love with Vennard's looks she might fall in love with his own. Being a philosopher in his way, he was content to take what the gods gave, and ask for no explanations.

I do not know how their conversation prospered, for my attention was distracted by the extraordinary behaviour of the Home Secretary. Mr. Cargill had made himself notorious by his treatment of "political" prisoners. It was sufficient in his eyes for a criminal to confess to political convictions to secure the most lenient treatment and a speedy release. The Irish patriot who cracked skulls in the Scotland Division of Liverpool, the Suffragist who broke windows and the noses of the police, the Social Democrat whose antipathy to the Tsar revealed itself in assaults upon the Russian Embassy, the "hunger-marchers" who had designs on the British Museum,--all were sure of respectful and tender handling. He had announced more than once, amid tumultuous cheering, that he would never be the means of branding earnestness, however mistaken, with the badge of the felon.

He was talking I recall, to Lady Lavinia Dobson, renowned in two hemispheres for her advocacy of women's rights. And this was what I heard him say. His face had grown suddenly flushed and his eye bright, so that he looked liker than ever to a bookmaker who had had a good meeting. "No, no, my dear lady, I have been a lawyer, and it is my duty in office to see that the law, the palladium of British liberties is kept sacrosanct. The law is no respecter of persons, and I intend that it shall be no respecter of creeds. If men or women break the laws, to jail they shall go, though their intentions were those of the Apostle Paul. We don't punish them for being Socialists or Suffragists, but for breaking the peace. Why, goodness me, if we didn't, we should have every malefactor in Britain claiming preferential treatment because he was a Christian Scientist or a Pentecostal Dancer."

"Mr. Cargill, do you realise what you are saying?" said Lady Lavinia with a scared face.

"Of course I do. I am a lawyer, and may be presumed to know the law. If any other doctrine were admitted, the Empire would burst up in a fortnight."

"That I should live to hear you name that accursed name!" cried the outraged lady. "You are denying your gods, Mr. Cargill. You are forgetting the principles of a lifetime."

Mr. Cargill was becoming excited, and exchanging his ordinary Edinburgh-English for a broader and more effective dialect.

"Tut, tut, my good wumman, I may be allowed to know my own principles best. I tell ye I've always maintained these views from the day when I first walked the floor of the Parliament House. Besides, even if I hadn't, I'm surely at liberty to change if I get more light. Whoever makes a fetish of consistency is a trumpery body and little use to God or man. What ails ye at the Empire, too? Is it not better to have a big country than a kailyard, or a house in Grosvenor Square than a but-and-ben in Balham?"

Lady Lavinia folded her hands. "We slaughter our black fellow-citizens, we fill South Africa with yellow slaves, we crowd the Indian prisons with the noblest and most enlightened of the Indian race, and we call it Empire building!"

"No, we don't," said Mr. Cargill stoutly, "we call it common-sense. That is the penal and repressive side of any great activity. D'ye mean to tell me that you never give your maid a good hearing? But would you like it to be said that you spent the whole of your days swearing at the wumman?"

"I never swore in my life," said Lady Lavinia.

"I spoke metaphorically," said Mr. Cargill. "If ye cannot understand a simple metaphor, ye cannot understand the rudiments of politics."

Picture to yourself a prophet who suddenly discovers that his God is laughing at him, a devotee whose saint winks and tells him that the devotion of years has been a farce, and you will get some idea of Lady Lavinia's frame of mind. Her sallow face flushed, her lip trembled, and she slewed round as far as her chair would permit her. Meanwhile Mr. Cargill, redder than before, went on contentedly with his dinner.

I was glad when my aunt gave the signal to rise. The atmosphere was electric, and all were conscious of it save the three Ministers, Deloraine, and Miss Claudia. Vennard seemed to be behaving very badly. He was arguing with Caerlaverock down the table, and the ex-Viceroy's face was slowly getting purple. When the ladies had gone, we remained oblivious to wine and cigarettes, listening to this heated controversy which threatened any minute to end in a quarrel.

The subject was India, and Vennard was discussing on the follies of all Viceroys.

"Take this idiot we've got now," he declared. "He expects me to be a sort of wet-nurse to the Government of India and do all their dirty work for them. They know local conditions, and they have ample powers if they would only use them, but they won't take an atom of responsibility. How the deuce am I to decide for them, when in the nature of things I can't be half as well informed about the facts!"

"Do you maintain," said Caerlaverock, stuttering in his wrath, "that the British Government should divest itself of responsibility for the governement of our great Indian Dependency?"

"Not a bit," said Vennard impatiently; "of course we are responsible, but that is all the more reason why the fellows who know the business at first hand should do their duty. If I am the head of a bank I am responsible for its policy, but that doesn't mean that every local bank-manager should consult me about the solvency of clients I never heard of. Faversham keeps bleating to me that the state of India is dangerous. Well, for God's sake let him suppress every native paper, shut up the schools, and send every agitator to the Andamans. I'll back him up all right. But don't let him ask me what to do, for I don't know."

"You think such a course would be popular?" asked a large, grave man, a newspaper editor.

"Of course it would," said Vennard cheerily. "The British public hates the idea of letting India get out of hand. But they want a lead. They can't be expected to start the show any more than I can."

Lord Caerlaverock rose to join the ladies with an air of outraged dignity. Vennard pulled out his watch and announced that he must go back to the House.

"Do you know what I am going to do?" he asked. "I am going down to tell Simpson what I think of him. He gets up and prates of having been forty years in India. Well, I am going to tell him that it is to him and his forty-year lot that all this muddle is due. Oh, I assure you, there's going to be a row," said Vennard, as he struggled into his coat.

Mulross had been sitting next me, and I asked him if he was leaving town. "I wish I could," he said, "but I fear I must stick on over the Twelfth. I don't like the way that fellow Von Kladow has been talking. He's up to no good, and he's going to get a flea in his ear before he is very much older."

Cheerfully, almost hilariously the three Ministers departed, Vennard and Cargill in a hansom and Mulross on foot. I can only describe the condition of those left behind as nervous prostration. We looked furtively at each other, each afraid to hint his suspicions, but all convinced that a surprising judgment had befallen at least two members of his Majesty's Government. For myself I put the number at three, for I did not like to hear a respected Whig Foreign Secretary talk about giving the Chancellor of a friendly but jealous Power a flea in his ear.

The only unperplexed face was Deloraine's. He whispered to me that Miss Barriton was going on to the Alvanleys' ball, and had warned him to be there. "She hasn't been to a dance for months, you know," he said. "I really think things are beginning to go a little better, old man."

III

When I opened my paper next morning I read two startling pieces of news. Lord Mulross had been knocked down by a taxi-cab on his way home the night before, and was now in bed suffering from a bad shock and a bruised ankle. There was no cause for anxiety, said the report, but his lordship must keep his room for a week or two.

The second item, which filled leading articles and overflowed into "Political Notes," was Mr. Vennard's speech. The Secretary for India had gone down about eleven o'clock to the House, where an Indian debate was dragging out its slow length. He sat himself on the Treasury Bench and took notes, and the House soon filled in anticipation of his reply. His "tail"--progressive young men like himself--were there in full strength, ready to cheer every syllable which fell from their idol. Somewhere about half-past twelve he rose to wind up the debate, and the House was treated to an unparalleled sensation. He began with his critics, notably the unfortunate Simpson, and, pretty much in Westbury's language to the herald, called them silly old men who did not understand their silly old business. But it was the reasons he gave for this abuse which left his followers aghast. He attacked his critics not for being satraps and reactionaries, but because they had dared to talk second-rate Western politics in connection with India.

"Have you lived for forty years with your eyes shut," he cried, "that you cannot see the difference between a Bengali, married at fifteen and worshipping a pantheon of savage gods, and the university-extension Young Radical at home? There is a thousand years between them, and you dream of annihilating the centuries with a little dubious popular science!" Then he turned to the other critics of Indian administration--his quondam supporters. He analysed the character of these " members for India" with a vigour and acumen which deprived them of speech. The East, he said, had had its revenge upon the West by making certain Englishmen babus. His honourable friends had the same slipshod minds, and they talked the same pigeon-English, as the patriots of Bengal. Then his mood changed, and he delivered a solemn warning against what he called "the treason begotten of restless vanity and proved incompetence." He sat down, leaving a House deeply impressed and horribly mystified.

The Times did not know what to make of it at all. In a weighty leader it welcomed Mr. Vennard's conversion, but hinted that with a convert's zeal he had slightly overstated his case. The Daily Chronicle talked of "nervous breakdown," and suggested "kindly forgetfulness" as the best treatment. The Daily News, in a spirited article called "The Great Betrayal," washed its hands of Mr. Vennard unless he donned the white sheet of the penitent. Later in the day I got The Westminster Gazette, and found an ingenious leader which proved that the speech in no way conflicted with Liberal principles, and was capable of a quite ordinary explanation. Then I went to see Lady Caerlaverock.

I found my aunt almost in tears.

"What has happened?" she cried. "What have we done that we should be punished in this awful way? And to think that the blow fell in this house? Caerlaverock--we all--thought Mr. Vennard so strange last night, and Lady Lavinia told me that Mr. Cargill was perfectly horrible. I suppose it must be the heat and the strain of the session. And that poor Lord Mulross, who was always so wise, should be stricken down at this crisis!"

I did not say that I thought Mulross's accident a merciful dispensation. I was far more afraid of him than of all the others, for if with his reputation for sanity he chose to run amok, he would be taken seriously. He was better in bed than affixing a flea to Von Kladow's ear.

"Caerlaverock was with the Prime Minister this morning," my aunt went on. "He is going to make a statement in the Lords tomorrow to try to cover Mr. Vennard's folly. They are very anxious about what Mr. Cargill will do today. He is addressing the National Convention of Young Liberals at Oldham this afternoon, and though they have sent him a dozen telegrams they can get no answer. Caerlaverock went to Downing Street an hour ago to get news."

There was the sound of an electric brougham stopping in the square below, and we both listened with a premonition of disaster. A minute later Caerlaverock entered the room, and with him the Prime Minister. The cheerful, eupeptic countenance of the latter was clouded with care. He shook hands dismally with my aunt, nodded to me, and flung himself down on a sofa.

"The worst has happened," Caerlaverock boomed solemnly. "Cargill has been incredibly and infamously silly." He tossed me an evening paper.

One glance convinced me that the Convention of Young Liberals had had a waking-up. Cargill had addressed them on what he called the true view of citizenship. He had dismissed manhood suffrage as an obsolete folly. The franchise, he maintained, should be narrowed and given only to citizens, and his definition of citizenship was military training combined with a fairly high standard of rates and taxes. I do not know how the Young Liberals received his creed, but it had no sort of success with the Prime Minister.

"We must disavow him," said Caerlaverock.

"He is too valuable a man to lose," said the Prime Minister. "We must hope that it is only a temporary aberration. I simply cannot spare him in the House."

"But this is flat treason."

"I know, I know. It is all too horrible, and utterly unexpected. But the situation wants delicate handling, my dear Caerlaverock. I see nothing for it but to give out that he was ill."

"Or drunk?" I suggested.

The Prime Minister shook his head sadly. "I fear it will be the same thing. What we call illness the ordinary man will interpret as intoxication. It is a most regrettable necessity, but we must face it."

The harassed leader rose, seized the evening paper, and departed as swiftly as he had come. "Remember, illness," were his parting words. "An old heart trouble, which is apt to affect his brain. His friends have always known about it."

I walked home, and looked in at the Club on my way. There I found Deloraine devouring a hearty tea and looking the picture of virtuous happiness.

"Well, this is tremendous news," I said, as I sat down beside him.

"What news?" he asked with a start.

"This row about Vennard and Cargill."

"Oh, that! I haven't seen the papers to-day. What's it all about?" His tone was devoid of interest.

Then I knew that something of great private moment had happened to Tommy.

"I hope I may congratulate you," I said.

Deloraine beamed on me affectionately. "Thanks very much, old man. Things came all right, quite suddenly, you know. We spent most of the time at the Alvanleys together, and this morning in the Park she accepted me. It will be in the papers next week, but we mean to keep it quiet for a day or two. However, it was your right to be told--and, besides,you guessed."

I remember wondering, as I finished my walk home, whether there could not be some connection between the stroke of Providence which had driven three Cabinet Ministers demented and that gentler touch which had restored Miss Claudia Barriton to good sense and a reasonable marriage.

IV

The next week was an epoch in my life. I seemed to live in the centre of a Mad Tea-party, where every one was convinced of the madness, and yet resolutely protested that nothing had happened. The public events of those days were simple enough. While Lord Mulross's ankle approached convalescence, the hives of politics were humming with rumours. Vennard's speech had dissolved his party into its parent elements, and the Opposition, as nonplussed as the Government, did not dare as yet to claim the recruit. Consequently he was left alone till he should see fit to take a further step. He refused to be interviewed, using blasphemous language about our free Press; and mercifully he showed no desire to make speeches. He went down to golf at Littlestone, and rarely showed himself in the House. The earnest young reformer seemed to have adopted not only the creed but the habits of his enemies.

Mr. Cargill's was a hard case. He returned from Oldham, delighted with himself and full of fight, to find awaiting him an urgent message from the Prime Minister. His chief was sympathetic and kindly. He had long noticed that the Home Secretary looked fagged and ill. There was no Home Office Bill very pressing, and his assistance in general debate could be dispensed with for a little. Let him take a fortnight's holiday--fish, golf, yacht--the Prime Minister was airily suggestive. In vain Mr. Cargill declared he was perfectly well. His chief gently but firmly overbore him, and insisted on sending him his own doctor. That eminent specialist, having been well coached, was vaguely alarming, and insisted on a change. Then Mr. Cargill began to suspect, and asked the Prime Minister point-blank if he objected to his Oldham speech. He was told that there was no objection--a little strong meat, perhaps, for Young Liberals, a little daring, but full of Mr. Cargill's old intellectual power. Mollified and reassured, the Home Secretary agreed to a week's absence, and departed for a little salmon-fishing in Scotland. His wife had meantime been taken into the affair, and privately assured by the Prime Minister that she would greatly ease the mind of the Cabinet if she could induce her husband to take a longer holiday--say three weeks. She promised to do her best and to keep her instructions secret, and the Cargills duly departed for the North. "In a fortnight," said the Prime Minister to my aunt, "he will have forgotten all this nonsense; but of course we shall have to watch him very carefully in the future."

The Press was given its cue, and announced that Mr. Cargill had spoken at Oldham while suffering from severe nervous breakdown, and that the remarkable doctrines of that speech need not be taken seriously. As I had expected, the public put its own interpretation upon this tale. Men took each other aside in clubs, women gossiped in drawing-rooms, and in a week the Cargill scandal had assumed amazing proportions. The popular version was that the Home Secretary had got very drunk at Caerlaverock House, and still under the influence of liquor had addressed the Young Liberals at Oldham. He was now in an Inebriates' Home, and would not return to the House that session. I confess I trembled when I heard this story, for it was altogether too libellous to pass unnoticed. I believed that soon it would reach the ear of Cargill, fishing quietly at Tomandhoul, and that then there would be the deuce to pay.

Nor was I wrong. A few days later I went to see my aunt to find out how the land lay. She was very bitter, I remember, about Claudia Barriton. "I expected sympathy and help from her, and she never comes near me. I can understand her being absorbed in her engagement, but I cannot understand the frivolous way she spoke when I saw her yesterday. She had the audacity to say that both Mr. Vennard and Mr. Cargill had gone up in her estimation. Young people can be so heartless."

I would have defended Miss Barriton, but at this moment an astonishing figure was announced. It was Mrs. Cargill in travelling dress, with a purple bonnet and a green motor-veil. Her face was scarlet, whether from excitement or the winds of Tomandhoul, and she charged down on us like a young bull.

"We have come back," she said, "to meet our accusers. "

"Accusers!" cried my aunt.

"Yes, accusers!" said the lady. "The abominable rumour about Alexander has reached our ears. At this moment he is with the Prime Minister, demanding an official denial. I have come to you, because it was here, at your table, that Alexander is said to have fallen."

"I really don't know what you mean, Mrs. Cargill."

"I mean that Alexander is said to have become drunk while dining here, to have been drunk when he spoke at Oldham, and to be now in a Drunkard's Home." The poor lady broke down, "Alexander," she cried, "who has been a teetotaller from his youth, and for thirty years an elder in the U.P. Church! No form of intoxicant has ever been permitted at our table. Even in illness the thing has never passed our lips."

My aunt by this time had pulled herself together. "If this outrageous story is current, Mrs. Cargill, there was nothing for it but to come back. Your friends know that it is a gross libel. The only denial necessary is for Mr. Cargill to resume his work. I trust his health is better."

"He is well, but heartbroken. His is a sensitive nature, Lady Caerlaverock, and he feels a stain like a wound."

"There is no stain," said my aunt briskly. "Every public man is a target for scandals, but no one but a fool believes them. They will die a natural death when he returns to work. An official denial would make everybody look ridiculous, and encourage the ordinary person to think that there may have been something in them. Believe me, dear Mrs. Cargill, there is nothing to be anxious about now that you are back in London again."

On the contrary, I thought, there was more cause for anxiety than ever. Cargill was back in the House and the illness game could not be played a second time. I went home that night acutely sympathetic towards the worries of the Prime Minister. Mulross would be abroad in a day or two, and Vennard and Cargill were volcanoes in eruption. The Government was in a parlous state, with three demented Ministers on the loose.

The same night I first heard the story of The Bill. Vennard had done more than play golf at Littlestone. His active mind--for his bitterest enemies never denied his intellectual energy--had been busy on a great scheme. At that time, it will be remembered, a serious shrinkage of unskilled labour existed not only in the Transvaal, but in the new copper fields of East Africa. Simultaneously a famine was scourging Behar, and Vennard, to do him justice, had made manful efforts to cope with it. He had gone fully into the question, and had been slowly coming to the conclusion that Behar was hopelessly overcrowded. In his new frame of mind--unswervingly logical, utterly unemotional, and wholly unbound by tradition--he had come to connect the African and Indian troubles, and to see in one the relief of the other. The first fruit of his meditations was a letter to The Times. In it he laid down a new theory of emigration. The peoples of the Empire, he said, must be mobile, shifting about to suit economic conditions. But if this was true of the white man, it was equally true for the dark races under our tutelage. He referred to the famine and argued that the recurrence of such disasters was inevitable, unless we assisted the poverty-stricken ryot to emigrate and sell his labour to advantage. He proposed indentures and terminable contracts, for he declared he had no wish to transplant for good. All that was needed was a short season of wage-earning abroad, that the labourer might return home with savings which would set him for the future on a higher economic plane. The letter was temperate and academic in phrasing, the speculation of a publicist rather than the declaration of a Minister. But in Liberals, who remembered the pandemonium raised over the Chinese in South Africa, it stirred up the gloomiest forebodings.

Then, whispered from mouth to mouth, came the news of the Great Bill. Vennard, it was said, intended to bring in a measure at the earliest possible date to authorise a scheme of enforced and State-aided emigration to the African mines. It would apply at first only to the famine districts, but power would be given to extend its working by proclamation to other areas. Such was the rumour, and I need not say it was soon magnified. Questions were asked in the House which the Speaker ruled out of order. Furious articles, inviting denial, appeared in the Liberal Press; but Vennard took not the slightest notice. He spent his time between his office in Whitehall and the links at Littlestone, dropping into the House once or twice for half an hour's slumber while a colleague was speaking. His Under Secretary in the Lords--a young gentleman who had joined the party for a bet, and to his immense disgust had been immediately rewarded with office--lost his temper under cross-examination and swore audibly at the Opposition. In a day or two the story universally believed was that the Secretary for India was about to transfer the bulk of the Indian people to work as indentured labourers for South African Jews.

It was this popular version, I fancy, which reached the ears of Ram Singh, and the news came on him like a thunderclap. He thought that what Vennard proposed Vennard could do. He saw his native province stripped of its people, his fields left unploughed, and his cattle untended; nay, it was possible, his own worthy and honourable self sent to a far country to dig in a hole. It was a grievous and intolerable prospect. He walked home to Gloucester Road in heavy preoccupation, and the first thing he did was to get out the mysterious brass box in which he kept his valuables. From a pocket-book he took a small silk packet, opened it, and spilled a few clear grains on his hand. It was the antidote.

He waited two days, while on all sides the rumour of the Bill grew stronger and its provisions more stringent. Then he hesitated no longer, but sent for Lord Caerlaverock's cook.

V

I conceive that the drug did not create new opinions, but elicited those which had hitherto lain dormant. Every man has a creed, but in his soul he knows that that creed has another side, possibly not less logical, which it does not suit him to produce. Our most honest convictions are not the children of pure reason, but of temperament, environment, necessity, and interest. Most of us take sides in life and forget the one we reject. But our conscience tells us it is there, and we can on occasion state it with a fairness and fulness which proves that it is not wholly repellent to our reason. During the crisis I write of, the attitude of Cargill and Vennard was not that of roysterers out for irresponsible mischief. They were eminently reasonable and wonderfully logical, and in private conversation they gave their opponents a very bad time. Cargill, who had hitherto been the hope of the extreme Free-traders, wrote an article for the Quarterly on Tariff Reform. It was set up, but long before it could be used it was cancelled and the type scattered. I have seen a proof of it, however, and I confess I have never read a more brilliant defence of a doctrine which the author had hitherto described as a childish heresy. Which proves my contention--that Cargill all along knew that there was a case against Free Trade, but naturally did not choose to admit it, his allegiance being vowed elsewhere. The drug altered temperament, and with it the creed which is based mainly on temperament. It scattered current convictions, roused dormant speculations, and without damaging the reason switched it on to a new track.

I can see all this now, but at the time I saw only stark madness and the horrible ingenuity of the lunatic. While Vennard was ruminating on his Bill, Cargill was going about London arguing like a Scotch undergraduate. The Prime Minister had seen from the start that the Home Secretary was the worse danger. Vennard might talk of his preposterous Bill, but the Cabinet would have something to say to it before its introduction, and he was mercifully disinclined to go near St. Stephen's. But Cargill was assiduous in his attendance at the House, and at any moment might blow the Government sky-high. His colleagues were detailed in relays to watch him. One would hale him to luncheon, and keep him till question time was over. Another would insist on taking him for a motor ride, which would end in a break-down about Brentford. Invitations to dinner were showered upon him, and Cargill, who had been unknown in society, found the whole social machinery of his party set at work to make him a lion. The result was that he was prevented from speaking in public, but given far too much encouragement to talk in private. He talked incessantly, before, at, and after dinner, and he did enormous harm. He was horribly clever, too, and usually got the best of an argument, so that various eminent private Liberals had their tempers ruined by his dialectic. In his rich and unabashed accent--he had long discarded his Edinburgh-English--he dissected their arguments and ridiculed their character. He had once been famous for his soapy manners: now he was as rough as a Highland stot.

Things could not go on in this fashion: the risk was too great. It was just a fortnight, I think, after the Caerlaverock dinner-party, when the Prime Minister resolved to bring matters to a head. He could not afford to wait for ever on a return of sanity. He consulted Caerlaverock, and it was agreed that Vennard and Cargill should be asked, or rather commanded to dine on the following evening at Caerlaverock House. Mulross, whose sanity was not suspected, and whose ankle was now well again, was also invited, as were three other members of the Cabinet and myself as amicus curiae. It was understood that after dinner there would be a settling-up with the two rebels. Either they should recant and come to heel, or they should depart from the fold to swell the wolf-pack of the Opposition. The Prime Minister did not conceal the loss which his party would suffer, but he argued very sensibly that anything was better than a brace of vipers in its bosom.

I have never attended a more lugubrious function. When I arrived I found Caerlaverock, the Prime Minister, and the three other members of the Cabinet standing round a small fire in attitudes of nervous dejection. I remember it was a raw wet evening, but the gloom out of doors was sunshine compared to the gloom within. Caerlaverock's viceregal air had sadly altered. The Prime Minister, once famous for his genial manners, was pallid and preoccupied. We exchanged remarks about the weather and the duration of the session. Then we fell silent till Mulross arrived.

He did not look as if he had come from a sickbed. He came in as jaunty as a boy, limping just a little from his accident. He was greeted by his colleagues with tender solicitude,--solicitude, I fear, completely wasted on him.

"Devilish silly thing to do to get run over," he said. "I was in a brown study when a cab came round a corner. But I don't regret it, you know. During the last fortnight I have had leisure to go into this Bosnian Succession business, and I see now that Von Kladow has been playing one big game of bluff. Very well; it has got to stop. I am going to prick the bubble before I am many days older."

The Prime Minister looked anxious. "Our policy towards Bosnia has been one of non-interference. It is not for us, I should have thought, to read Germany a lesson."

"Oh, come now," Mulross said, slapping--yes, actually slapping-- his leader on the back; "we may drop that nonsense when we are alone. You know very well that there are limits to our game of non-interference. If we don't read Germany a lesson, she will read us one--and a damned long unpleasant one too. The sooner we give up all this milk-blooded, blue-spectacled, pacificist talk the better. However, you will see what I have got to say to-morrow in the House."

The Prime Minister's face lengthened. Mulross was not the pillar he had thought him, but a splintering reed. I saw that he agreed with me that this was the most dangerous of the lot.

Then Cargill and Vennard came in together. Both looking uncommonly fit, younger, trimmer, cleaner. Vennard, instead of his sloppy clothes and shaggy hair, was groomed like a Guardsman; had a large pearl-and-diamond solitaire in his shirt, and a white waistcoat with jewelled buttons. He had lost all his self-consciousness, grinned cheerfully at the others, warmed his hands at the fire, and cursed the weather. Cargill, too, had lost his sanctimonious look. There was a bloom of rustic health on his cheek, and a sparkle in his eye, so that he had the appearance of some rosy Scotch laird of Raeburn's painting. Both men wore an air of purpose and contentment .

Vennard turned at once on the Prime Minister. "Did you get my letter?" he asked. "No? Well, you'll find it waiting when you get home. We're all friends here, so I can tell you its contents. We must get rid of this ridiculous Radical 'tail.' They think they have the whip-hand of us; well, we have got to prove that we can do very well without them. They are a collection of confounded, treacherous, complacent prigs, but they have no grit in them, and will come to heel if we tackle them firmly. I respect an honest fanatic, but I do not respect those sentiment-mongers. They have the impudence to say that the country is with them. I tell you it is rank nonsense. If you take a strong hand with them, you'll double your popularity, and we'll come back next year with an increased majority. Cargill agrees with me."

The Prime Minister looked grave. "I am not prepared to discuss any policy of ostracism. What you call our 'tail' is a vital section of our party. Their creed may be one-sided, but it is none the less part of our mandate from the people."

"I want a leader who governs as well as reigns," said Vennard. "I believe in discipline, and you know as well as I do that the Rump is infernally out of hand."

"They are not the only members who fail in discipline."

Vennard grinned. "I suppose you mean Cargill and myself. But we are following the central lines of British policy. We are on your side, and we want to make your task easier."

Cargill suddenly began to laugh. "I don't want any ostracism. Leave them alone, and Vennard and I will undertake to give them such a time in the House that they will wish they had never been born. We'll make them resign in batches."

Dinner was announced, and, laughing uproariously, the two rebels went arm-in-arm into the dining-room.

Cargill was in tremendous form. He began to tell Scotch stories, memories of his old Parliament House days. He told them admirably, with a raciness of idiom which I had thought beyond him. They were long tales, and some were as broad as they were long, but Mr. Cargill disarmed criticism. His audience, rather scandalised at the start, were soon captured, and political troubles were forgotten in old-fashioned laughter. Even the Prime Minister's anxious face relaxed.

This lasted till the entree, the famous Caerlaverock curry.

As I have said, I was not in the secret, and did not detect the transition. As I partook of the dish I remember feeling a sudden giddiness and a slight nausea. The antidote, to those who had not taken the drug, must have been, I suppose, in the nature of a mild emetic. A mist seemed to obscure the faces of my fellow-guests, and slowly the tide of conversation ebbed away. First Vennard, then Cargill, became silent. I was feeling rather sick, and I noticed with some satisfaction that all our faces were a little green. I wondered casually if I had been poisoned.

The sensation passed, but the party had changed. More especially I was soon conscious that something had happened to the three Ministers. I noticed Mulross particularly, for he was my neighbour. The look of keenness and vitality had died out of him, and suddenly he seemed a rather old, rather tired man, very weary about the eyes.

I asked him if he felt seedy.

"No, not specially," he replied, "but that accident gave me a nasty shock."

"You should go off for a change," I said.

"I almost thimk I will," was the answer. "I had not meant to leave town till just before the Twelfth but I think I had better get away to Marienbad for a fortnight. There is nothing doing in the House, and work at the Office is at a standstill. Yes, I fancy I'll go abroad before the end of the week."

I caught the Prime Minister's eye and saw that he had forgotten the purpose of the dinner, being dimly conscious that that purpose was now idle. Cargill and Vennard had ceased to talk like rebels. The Home Secretary had subsided into his old, suave, phrasing self. The humour had gone out of his eye, and the looseness had returned to his lips. He was an older and more commonplace man, but harmless, quite harmless. Vennard, too, wore a new air, or rather had recaptured his old one. He was saying little, but his voice had lost its crispness and recovered its half-plaintive unction; his shoulders had a droop in them; once more he bristled with self-consciousness.

We others were still shaky from that detestable curry, and were so puzzled as to be acutely uncomfortable. Relief would come later, no doubt; for the present we were uneasy at this weird transformation. I saw the Prime Minister examining the two faces intently, and the result seemed to satisfy him. He sighed and looked at Caerlaverock, who smiled and nodded.

"What about that Bill of yours, Vennard?" he asked. "There have been a lot of stupid rumours."

"Bill?" Vennard said. "I know of no Bill. Now that my departmental work is over, I can give my whole soul to Cargill's Small Holdings. Do you mean that?"

"Yes, of course. There was some confusion in the popular mind, but the old arrangement holds. You and Cargill will put it through between you."

They began to talk about those weariful small holdings, and I ceased to listen. We left the dining-room and drifted to the library, where a fire tried to dispel the gloom of the weather. There was a feeling of deadly depression abroad, so that, for all its awkwardness, I would really have preferred the former Caerlaverock dinner. The Prime Minister was whispering to his host. I heard him say something about there being "the devil of a lot of explaining" before him.

Vennard and Cargill came last to the library, arm-in-arm as before.

"I should count it a greater honour," Vennard was saying, "to sweeten the lot of one toiler in England than to add a million miles to our territory. While one English household falls below the minimum scale of civic wellbeing, all talk of Empire is sin and folly." "Excellent!" said Mr. Cargill. Then I knew for certain that at last peace had descended upon the vexed tents of Israel.

THE SHORTER CATECHISM

(Revised Version)

When I was young and herdit sheep I read auld tales o' Wallace wight; My held was fou o' sangs and threip O' folk that feared nae mortal might. But noo I'm auld, and weel I ken We're made alike o' gowd and mire; There's saft bits in the stievest men, The bairnliest's got a spunk o' fire.

Sae hearken to me, lads, It's truth that I tell: There's nae man a' courage-- I ken by mysel'.

I've been an elder forty year: I've tried to keep the narrow way: I've walked afore the Lord in fear: I've never missed the kirk a day. I've read the Bible in and oot, (I ken the feck o't clean by hert). But, still and on, I sair misdoot I'm better noo than at the stert.

Sae hearken to me, lads, It's truth I maintain: Man's works are but rags, for I ken by my ain.

I hae a name for decent trade: I'll wager a' the countryside Wad sweer nae trustier man was made, The ford to soom, the bent to bide. But when it comes to coupin' horse, I'm just like a' that e'er was born; I fling my heels and tak' my course; I'd sell the minister the morn.

Sae hearken to me, lads, It's truth that I tell: There's nae man deid honest-- I ken by mysel'.

III

THE LEMNIAN

He pushed the matted locks from his brow as he peered into the mist. His hair was thick with salt, and his eyes smarted from the greenwood fire on the poop. The four slaves who crouched beside the thwarts-Carians with thin birdlike faces-were in a pitiable case, their hands blue with oar-weals and the lash marks on their shoulders beginning to gape from sun and sea. The Lemnian himself bore marks of ill usage. His cloak was still sopping, his eyes heavy with watching, and his lips black and cracked with thirst. Two days before the storm had caught him and swept his little craft into mid-Aegean. He was a sailor, come of sailor stock, and he had fought the gale manfully and well. But the sea had burst his waterjars, and the torments of drought had been added to his toil. He had been driven south almost to Scyros, but had found no harbour. Then a weary day with the oars had brought him close to the Euboean shore, when a freshet of storm drove him seaward again. Now at last in this northerly creek of Sciathos he had found shelter and a spring. But it was a perilous place, for there were robbers in the bushy hills-mainland men who loved above all things to rob an islander: and out at sea, as he looked towards Pelion, there seemed something adoing which boded little good. There was deep water beneath a ledge of cliff, half covered by a tangle of wildwood. So Atta lay in the bows, looking through the trails of vine at the racing tides now reddening in the dawn.

The storm had hit others besides him it seemed. The channel was full of ships, aimless ships that tossed between tide and wind. Looking closer, he saw that they were all wreckage. There had been tremendous doings in the north, and a navy of some sort had come to grief. Atta was a prudent man, and knew that a broken fleet might be dangerous. There might be men lurking in the maimed galleys who would make short work of the owner of a battered but navigable craft. At first he thought that the ships were those of the Hellenes. The troublesome fellows were everywhere in the islands, stirring up strife and robbing the old lords. But the tides running strongly from the east were bringing some of the wreckage in an eddy into the bay. He lay closer and watched the spars and splintered poops as they neared him. These were no galleys of the Hellenes. Then came a drowned man, swollen and horrible: then another-swarthy, hooknosed fellows, all yellow with the sea. Atta was puzzled. They must be the men from the East about whom he had been hearing. Long ere he left Lemnos there had been news about the Persians. They were coming like locusts out of the dawn, swarming over Ionia and Thrace, men and ships numerous beyond telling. They meant no ill to honest islanders: a little earth and water were enough to win their friendship. But they meant death to the hubris of the Hellenes. Atta was on the side of the invaders; he wished them well in their war with his ancient foes. They would eat them up, Athenians, Lacedaemonians, Corinthians, Aeginetans, men of Argos and Elis, and none would be left to trouble him. But in the meantime something had gone wrong. Clearly there had been no battle. As the bodies butted against the side of the galley he hooked up one or two and found no trace of a wound. Poseidon had grown cranky, and had claimed victims. The god would be appeased by this time, and all would go well.

Danger being past, he bade the men get ashore and fill the water-skins. "God's curse on all Hellenes," he said, as he soaked up the cold water from the spring in the thicket.

About noon he set sail again. The wind sat in the north-east, but the wall of Pelion turned it into a light stern breeze which carried him swiftly westward. The four slaves, still leg-weary and arm-weary, lay like logs beside the thwarts. Two slept; one munched some salty figs; the fourth, the headman, stared wearily forward, with ever and again a glance back at his master. But the Lemnian never looked his way. His head was on his breast, as he steered, and he brooded on the sins of the Hellenes. He was of the old Pelasgian stock, the first bords of the land, who had come out of the soil at the call of God. The pillaging northmen had crushed his folk out of the mainlands and most of the islands, but in Lemnos they had met their match. It was a family story how every grown male had been slain, and how the women long after had slaughtered their conquerors in the night. "Lemnian deeds," said the Hellenes, when they wished to speak of some shameful thing: but to Atta the shame was a glory to be cherished for ever. He and his kind were the ancient people, and the gods loved old things, as those new folk would find. Very especially he hated the men of Athens. Had not one of their captains, Militades, beaten the Lemnians and brought the island under Athenian sway? True, it was a rule only in name, for any Athenian who came alone to Lemnos would soon be cleaving the air from the highest cliff-top. But the thought irked his pride, and he gloated over the Persians' coming. The Great King from beyond the deserts would smite those outrageous upstarts. Atta would willingly give earth and water. It was the whim of a fantastic barbarian, and would be well repaid if the bastard Hellenes were destroyed. They spoke his own tongue, and worshipped his own gods, and yet did evil. Let the nemesis of Zeus devour them!

The wreckage pursued him everywhere. Dead men shouldered the sides of the galley, and the straits were stuck full of things like monstrous buoys, where tall ships had foundered. At Artemision he thought he saw signs of an anchored fleet with the low poops of the

Hellenes, and sheered off to the northern shores. There, looking towards Oeta and the Malian Gulf, he found an anchorage at sunset. The waters were ugly and the times ill, and he had come on an enterprise bigger than he had dreamed. The Lemnian was a stout fellow, but he had no love for needless danger. He laughed mirthlessly as he thought of his errand, for he was going to Hellas, to the shrine of the Hellenes.

It was a woman's doing, like most crazy enterprises. Three years ago his wife had laboured hard in childbirth, and had had the whims of labouring women. Up in the keep of Larisa, on the windy hillside, there had been heart-searching and talk about the gods. The little olive-wood Hermes, the very private and particular god of Atta's folk, was good enough in simple things like a lambing or a harvest, but he was scarcely fit for heavy tasks. Atta's wife declared that her lord lacked piety. There were mainland gods who repaid worship, but his scorn of all Hellenes made him blind to the merits of those potent divinities. At first Atta resisted. There was Attic blood in his wife, and he strove to argue with her unorthodox craving. But the woman persisted, and a Lemnian wife, as she is beyond other wives in virtue and comeliness, excels them in stubbornness of temper. A second time she was with child, and nothing would content her but that Atta should make his prayers to the stronger gods. Dodona was far away, and long ere he reached it his throat would be cut in the hills. But Delphi was but two days' journey from the Malian coast, and the god of Delphi, the Far-Darter had surprising gifts, if one were to credit travellers' tales. Atta yielded with an ill grace, and out of his wealth devised an offering to Apollo. So on this July day he found himself looking across the gulf to Kallidromos bound for a Hellenic shrine, but hating all Hellenes in his soul. A verse of Homer consoled him—the words which Phocion spoke to Achilles. "Verily even the gods may be turned, they whose excellence and honour and strength are greater than thine; yet even these do men, when they pray, turn from their purpose with offerings of incense and pleasant vows." The Far-Darter must hate the hubris of those Hellenes, and be the more ready to avenge it since they dared to claim his countenance. "No race has ownership in the gods," a Lemnian song-maker had said when Atta had been questioning the ways of Poseidon.

The following dawn found him coasting past the north end of Euboea in the thin fog of a windless summer morn. He steered by the peak of Othrys and a spur of Oeta, as he had learnt from a slave who had travelled the road. Presently he was in the muddy Malian waters, and the sun was scattering the mist on the landward side. And then he became aware of a greater commotion than Poseidon's play with the ships off Pelion. A murmur like a winter's storm came seawards. He lowered the sail, which he had set to catch a chance breeze, and bade the men rest on their oars. An earthquake seemed to be tearing at the roots of the hills.

The mist rolled up, and his hawk eyes saw a strange sight. The water was green and still around him, but shoreward it changed its colour. It was a dirty red, and things bobbed about in it like the Persians in the creek of Sciathos. On the strip of shore, below the sheer wall of Kallidromos, men were fighting-myriads of men, for away towards Locris they stretched in ranks and banners and tents till the eye lost them in the haze. There was no sail on the queer, muddy-red-edged sea; there was no man on the hills: but on that one flat ribbon of sand all the nations of the earth were warring. He remembered about the place: Thermopylae they called it, the Gate of the Hot Springs. The Hellenes were fighting the Persians in the pass for their Fatherland.

Atta was prudent and loved not other men's quarrels. He gave the word to the rowers to row seaward. In twenty strokes they were in the mist again...

Atta was prudent, but he was also stubborn. He spent the day in a creek on the northern shore of the gulf, listening to the weird hum which came over the waters out of the haze. He cursed the delay. Up on Kallidromos would be clear dry air and the path to Delphi among the oak woods. The Hellenes could not be fighting everywhere at once. He might find some spot on the shore, far in their rear, where he could land and gain the hills. There was danger indeed, but once on the ridge he would be safe; and by the time he came back the Great King would have swept the defenders into the sea, and be well on the road for Athens. He asked himself if it were fitting that a Lemnian should be stayed in his holy task by the struggles of Hellene and Barbarian. His thoughts flew to his steading at Larisa, and the dark-eyed wife who was awaiting his homecoming. He could not return without Apollo's favour: his manhood and the memory of his lady's eyes forbade it. So late in the afternoon he pushed off again and steered his galley for the south.

About sunset the mist cleared from the sea; but the dark falls swiftly in the shadow of the high hills, and Atta had no fear. With the night the hum sank to a whisper; it seemed that the invaders were drawing off to camp, for the sound receded to the west. At the last light the Lemnian touched a rock-point well to the rear of the defence. He noticed that the spume at the tide's edge was reddish and stuck to his hands like gum. Of a surety much blood was flowing on that coast.

He bade his slaves return to the north shore and lie hidden to await him. When he came back he would light a signal fire on the topmost bluff of Kallidromos. Let them watch for it and come to take him off. Then he seized his bow and quiver, and his short hunting-spear, buckled his cloak about him, saw that the gift to Apollo was safe in the folds of it, and marched sturdily up the hillside.

The moon was in her first quarter, a slim horn which at her rise showed only the faint outline of the hill. Atta plodded steadfastly on, but he found the way hard. This was not like the crisp sea-turf of Lemnos, where among the barrows of the ancient dead, sheep and kine could find sweet fodder. Kallidromos ran up as steep as the roof of a barn. Cytisus and thyme and juniper grew rank, but above all the place was strewn with rocks, leg-twisting boulders, and great cliffs where eagles dwelt. Being a seaman, Atta had his bearings. The path to Delphi left the shore road near the Hot Springs, and went south by a rift of the mountain. If he went up the slope in a beeline he must strike it in time and find better going. Still it was an eerie place to be tramping after dark. The Hellenes had strange gods of the thicket and hillside, and he had no wish to intrude upon their sanctuaries. He told himself that next to the Hellenes he hated this country of theirs, where a man sweltered in hot jungles or tripped among hidden crags. He sighed for the cool beaches below Larisa, where the surf was white as the snows of Samothrace, and the fisherboys sang round their smoking broth-pots.

Presently he found a path. It was not the mule road, worn by many feet, that he had looked for, but a little track which twined among the boulders. Still it eased his feet, so he cleared the thorns from his sandals, strapped his belt tighter, and stepped out more confidently. Up and up he went, making odd detours among the crags. Once he came to a promontory, and, looking down, saw lights twinkling from the Hot Springs. He had thought the course lay more southerly, but consoled himself by remembering that a mountain path must have many windings. The great matter was that he was ascending, for he knew that he must cross the ridge of Oeta before he struck the Locrian glens that led to the Far-Darter's shrine.

At what seemed the summit of the first ridge he halted for breath, and, prone on the thyme, looked back to sea. The Hot Springs were hidden, but across the gulf a single light shone from the far shore. He guessed that by this time his galley had been beached and his slaves were cooking supper. The thought made him homesick. He had beaten and cursed these slaves of his times without number, but now in this strange land he felt them kinsfolk, men of his own household. Then he told himself he was no better than a woman. Had he not gone sailing to Chalcedon and distant Pontus, many months' journey from home while this was but a trip of days? In a week he would be welcomed by a smiling wife, with a friendly god behind him.

The track still bore west, though Delphi lay in the south. Moreover, he had come to a broader road running through a little tableland. The highest peaks of Oeta were dark against the sky, and around him was a flat glade where oaks whispered in the night breezes. By this time he judged from the stars that midnight had passed, and he began to consider whether, now that he was beyond the fighting, he should not sleep and wait for dawn. He made up his mind to find a shelter, and, in the aimless way of the night traveller, pushed on and on in the quest of it. The truth is his mind was on Lemnos, and a dark-eyed, white-armed dame spinning in the evening by the threshold. His eyes roamed among the oaktrees, but vacantly and idly, and many a mossy corner was passed unheeded. He forgot his ill temper, and hummed cheerfully the song his reapers sang in the barley-fields below his orchard. It was a song of seamen turned husbandmen, for the gods it called on were the gods of the sea....

Suddenly he found himself crouching among the young oaks, peering and listening. There was something coming from the west. It was like the first mutterings of a storm in a narrow harbour, a steady rustling and whispering. It was not wind; he knew winds too well to be deceived. It was the tramp of light-shod feet among the twigs--many feet, for the sound remained steady, while the noise of a few men will rise and fall. They were coming fast and coming silently. The war had reached far up Kallidromos.

Atta had played this game often in the little island wars. Very swiftly he ran back and away from the path up the slope which he knew to be the first ridge of Kallidromos. The army, whatever it might be, was on the Delphian road. Were the Hellenes about to turn the flank of the Great King?

A moment later he laughed at his folly. For the men began to appear, and they were crossing to meet him, coming from the west. Lying close in the brushwood he could see them clearly. It was well he had left the road, for they stuck to it, following every winding-crouching, too, like hunters after deer. The first man he saw was a Hellene, but the ranks behind were no Hellenes. There was no glint of bronze or gleam of fair skin. They were dark, long-haired fellows, with spears like his own, and round Eastern caps, and egg-shaped bucklers. Then Atta rejoiced. It was the Great King who was turning the flank of the Hellenes. They guarded the gate, the fools, while the enemy slipped through the roof.

He did not rejoice long. The van of the army was narrow and kept to the path, but the men behind were straggling all over the hillside. Another minute and he would be discovered. The thought was cheerless. It was true that he was an islander and friendly to the Persian, but up on the heights who would listen to his tale? He would be taken for a spy, and one of those thirsty spears would drink his blood. It must be farewell to Delphi for the moment, he thought, or farewell to Lemnos for ever. Crouching low, he ran back and away from the path to the crest of the sea-ridge of Kallidromos.

The men came no nearer him. They were keeping roughly to the line of the path, and drifted through the oak wood before him, an army without end. He had scarcely thought there were so many fighting men in the world. He resolved to lie there on the crest, in the hope that ere the first light they would be gone. Then he would push on to Delphi, leaving them to settle their quarrels behind him. These were the hard times for a pious pilgrim.

But another noise caught his ear from the right. The army had flanking squadrons, and men were coming along the ridge. Very bitter anger rose in Atta's heart. He had cursed the Hellenes, and now he cursed the Barbarians no less. Nay, he cursed all war, that spoiled the errands of peaceful folk. And then, seeking safety, he dropped over the crest on to the steep shoreward face of the mountain.

In an instant his breath had gone from him. He slid down a long slope of screes, and then with a gasp found himself falling sheer into space. Another second and he was caught in a tangle of bush, and then dropped once more upon screes, where he clutched desperately for handhold. Breathless and bleeding he came to anchor on a shelf of greensward and found himself blinking up at the crest which seemed to tower a thousand feet above. There were men on the crest now. He heard them speak and felt that they were looking down.

The shock kept him still till the men had passed. Then the terror of the place gripped him, and he tried feverishly to retrace his steps. A dweller all his days among gentle downs, he grew dizzy with the sense of being hung in space. But the only fruit of his efforts was to set him slipping again. This time he pulled up at the root of gnarled oak, which overhung the sheerest cliff on Kallidromos. The danger brought his wits back. He sullenly reviewed his case, and found it desperate.

He could not go back, and, even if he did, he would meet the Persians. If he went on he would break his neck, or at the best fall into the Hellenes' hands. Oddly enough he feared his old enemies less than his friends. He did not think that the Hellenes would butcher him. Again, he might sit perched in his eyrie till they settled their quarrel, or he fell off. He rejected this last way. Fall off he should for certain, unless he kept moving. Already he was retching with the vertigo of the heights. It was

THE MOON ENDURETH

growing lighter. Suddenly he was looking not into a black world, but to a pearl-grey floor far beneath him. It was the sea, the thing he knew and loved. The sight screwed up his courage. He remembered that he was Lemnian and a seafarer. He would be conquered neither by rock, nor by Hellene, nor by the Great King. Least of all by the last, who was a barbarian. Slowly, with clenched teeth and narrowed eyes, he began to clamber down a ridge which flanked the great cliffs of Kallidromos. His plan was to reach the shore and take the road to the east before the Persians completed their circuit. Some instinct told him that a great army would not take the track he had mounted by. There must be some longer and easier way debouching farther down the coast. He might yet have the good luck to slip between them and the sea.

The two hours which followed tried his courage hard. Thrice he fell, and only a juniper-root stood between him and death. His hands grew ragged, and his nails were worn to the quick. He had long ago lost his weapons; his cloak was in shreds, all save the breast-fold which held the gift to Apollo. The heavens brightened, but he dared not look around. He knew he was traversing awesome places, where a goat could scarcely tread. Many times he gave up hope of life. His head was swimming, and he was so deadly sick that often he had to lie gasping on some shoulder of rock less steep than the rest. But his anger kept him to his purpose. He was filled with fury at the Hellenes. It was they and their folly that had brought him these mischances. Some day ....

He found himself sitting blinking on the shore of the sea. A furlong off the water was lapping on the reefs. A man, larger than human in the morning mist, was standing above him.

"Greeting, stranger," said the voice. "By Hermes, you choose the difficult roads to travel."

Atta felt for broken bones, and, reassured, struggled to his feet.

"God's curse upon all mountains," he said. He staggered to the edge of the tide and laved his brow. The savour of salt revived him. He turned to find the tall man at his elbow, and noted how worn and ragged he was, and yet how upright. "When a pigeon is flushed from the rocks, there is a hawk near," said the voice.

Atta was angry. "A hawk!" he cried. "Nay, an army of eagles. There will be some rare flushing of Hellenes before evening."

"What frightened you, Islander?" the stranger asked. "Did a wolf bark up on the hillside?"

"Ay, a wolf. The wolf from the East with a multitude of wolflings. There will be fine eating soon in the pass."

The man's face grew dark. He put his hand to his mouth and called. Half a dozen sentries ran to join him. He spoke to them in the harsh Lacedaemonian speech which made Atta sick to hear. They talked with the back of the throat and there was not an "s" in their words.

"There is mischief in the hills," the first man said. "This islander has been frightened down over the rocks. The Persian is stealing a march on us."

The sentries laughed. One quoted a proverb about island courage. Atta's wrath flared and he forgot himself. He had no wish to warn the Hellenes, but it irked his pride to be thought a liar. He began to tell his story hastily, angrily, confusedly; and the men still laughed.

Then he turned eastward and saw the proof before him. The light had grown and the sun was coming up over Pelion. The first beam fell on the eastern ridge of Kallidromos, and there, clear on the sky-line, was the proof. The Persian was making a wide circuit, but moving shoreward. In a little he would be at the coast, and by noon at the Hellenes' rear.

His hearers doubted no more. Atta was hurried forward through the lines of the Greeks to the narrow throat of the pass, where behind a rough rampart of stones lay the Lacedaemonian headquarters. He was still giddy from the heights, and it was in a giddy dream that he traversed the misty shingles of the beach amid ranks of sleeping warriors. It was a grim place, for there were dead and dying in it, and blood on every stone. But in the lee of the wall little fires were burning and slaves were cooking breakfast. The smell of roasting flesh came pleasantly to his nostrils, and he remembered that he had had no meal since he crossed the gulf.

Then he found himself the centre of a group who had the air of kings. They looked as if they had been years in war. Never had he seen faces so worn and so terribly scarred. The hollows in their cheeks gave them the air of smiling, and yet they were grave. Their scarlet vests were torn and muddled, and the armour which lay near was dinted like the scrap-iron before a smithy door. But what caught his attention were the eyes of the men. They glittered as no eyes he had ever seen before glittered. The sight cleared his bewilderment and took the pride out of his heart. He could not pretend to despise a folk who looked like Ares fresh from the wars of the Immortals.

They spoke among themselves in quiet voices. Scouts came and went, and once or twice one of the men, taller than the rest, asked Atta a question. The Lemnian sat in the heart of the group, sniffing the smell of cooking, and looking at the rents in his cloak and the long scratches on his legs. Something was pressing on his breast, and he found that it was Apollo's gift. He had forgotten all about it. Delphi seemed beyond the moon, and his errand a child's dream.

Then the King, for so he thought of the tall man, spoke--

"You have done us a service, Islander. The Persian is at our back and front, and there will be no escape for those who stay. Our allies are going home, for they do not share our vows. We of Lacedaemon wait in the pass. If you go with the men of Corinth you will find a place of safety before noon. No doubt in the Euripus there is some boat to take you to your own land."

He spoke courteously, not in the rude Athenian way; and somehow the quietness of his voice and his glittering eyes roused wild longings in Atta's heart. His island pride was face to face with a greater-greater than he had ever dreamed of.

"Bid yon cooks give me some broth," he said gruffly. "I am faint. After I have eaten I will speak with you."

He was given food, and as he ate he thought. He was on trial before these men of Lacedaemon. More, the old faith of the islands, the pride of the first masters, was at stake in his hands. He had boasted that he and his kind were the last of the men; now these Hellenes of Lacedaemon were preparing a great deed, and they deemed him unworthy to share in it. They offered him safety. Could he brook the insult? He had forgotten that the cause of the Persian was his; that the Hellenes were the foes of his race. He saw only that the last test of manhood was preparing and the manhood in him rose to greet the trial. An odd wild ecstasy surged in his veins. It was not the lust of battle, for he had no love of slaying, or hate for the Persian, for he was his friend. It was the sheer joy of proving that the Lemnian stock had a starker pride than these men of Lacedamon. They would die for their fatherland, and their vows; but he, for a whim, a scruple, a delicacy of honour. His mind was so clear that no other course occurred to him. There was only one way for a man. He, too, would be dying for his fatherland, for through him the island race would be ennobled in the eyes of gods and men.

Troops were filing fast to the east--Thebans, Corinthians. "Time flies, Islander," said the King's voice. "The hours of safety are slipping past." Atta looked up carelessly. "I will stay," he said. "God's curse on all Hellenes! Little I care for your quarrels. It is nothing to me if your Hellas is under the heels of the East. But I care much for brave men. It shall never be said that a man of Lemnos, a son of the old race, fell back when Death threatened. I stay with you, men of Lacedaemon."

The King's eyes glittered; they seemed to peer into his heart.

"It appears they breed men in the islands," he said. "But you err. Death does not threaten. Death awaits us."

"It is all one," said Atta. "But I crave a boon. Let me fight my last fight by your side. I am of older stock than you, and a king in my own country. I would strike my last blow among kings."

There was an hour of respite before battle was joined, and Atta spent it by the edge of the sea. He had been given arms, and in girding himself for the fight he had found Apollo's offering in his breastfold. He was done with the gods of the Hellenes. His offering should go to the gods of his own people. So, calling upon Poseidon, he flung the little gold cup far out to sea. It flashed in the sunlight, and then sank in the soft green tides so noiselessly that it seemed as if the hand of the Sea-god had been stretched to take it. "Hail, Poseidon!" the Lemnian cried. "I am bound this day for the Ferryman. To you only I make prayer, and to the little Hermes of Larisa. Be kind to my kin when they travel the sea, and keep them islanders and seafarers for ever. Hail and farewell, God of my own folk!"

Then, while the little waves lapped on the white sand, Atta made a song. He was thinking of the homestead far up in the green downs, looking over to the snows of Samothrace. At this hour in the morning there would be a tinkle of sheep-bells as the flocks went down to the low pastures. Cool wind would be blowing, and the noise of the surf below the cliffs would come faint to the ear. In the hall the maids mould be spinning, while their dark-haired mistress would be casting swift glances to the doorway, lest it might be filled any moment by the form of her returning lord. Outside in the chequered sunlight of the orchard the child would be playing with his nurse, crooning in childish syllables the chanty his father had taught him. And at the thought of his home a great passion welled up in Atta's heart. It was not regret, but joy and pride and aching love. In his antique island creed the death he was awaiting was not other than a bridal. He was dying for the things he loved, and by his death they would be blessed eternally. He would not have long to wait before bright eyes came to greet him in the House of Shadows.

So Atta made the Song of Atta, and sang it then, and later in the press of battle. It was a simple song, like the lays of seafarers. It put into rough verse the thought which cheers the heart of all adventurers--nay, which makes adventure possible for those who have much to leave. It spoke of the shining pathway of the sea which is the Great Uniter. A man may lie dead in Pontus or beyond the Pillars of Herakles, but if he dies on the shore there is nothing between him and his fatherland. It spoke of a battle all the long dark night in a strange place--a place of marshes and black cliffs and shadowy terrors.

"In the dawn the sweet light comes," said the song, "and the salt winds and the tides will bear me home..."

When in the evening the Persians took toll of the dead, they found one man who puzzled them. He lay among the tall Lacedaemonians on the very lip of the sea, and around him were swathes of their countrymen. It looked as if he had been fighting his way to the water, and had been overtaken by death as his feet reached the edge. Nowhere in the pass did the dead lie so thick, and yet he was no Hellene. He was torn like a deer that the dogs have worried, but the little left of his garments and his features spoke of Eastern race. The survivors could tell nothing except that he had fought like a god and had been singing all the while.

The matter came to the ear of the Great King who was sore enough at the issue of the day. That one of his men had performed feats of valeur beyond the Hellenes was a pleasant tale to tell. And so his captains reported it. Accordingly when the fleet from Artemision arrived next morning, and all but a few score Persians were shovelled into holes, that the Hellenes might seem to have been conquered by a lesser force, Atta's body was laid out with pomp in the midst of the Lacedaemonians. And the seamen rubbed their eyes and thanked their strange gods that one man of the East had been found to match those terrible warriors whose name was a nightmare. Further, the Great King gave orders that the body of Atta should be embalmed and carried with the army, and that his name and kin should be sought out and duly honoured. This latter was a task too hard for the staff, and no more was heard of it till months later, when the King, in full flight after Salamis, bethought him of the one man who had not played him false. Finding that his lieutenants had nothing to tell him, he eased five of them of their heads.

As it happened, the deed was not quite forgotten. An islander, a Lesbian and a cautious man, had fought at Therrnopylae in the Persian ranks, and had heard Atta's singing and seen how he fell. Long afterwards some errand took this man to Lemnos, and in the evening, speaking with the Elders, he told his tale and repeated something of the song. There was that in the words which gave the Lemnians a clue, the mention, I think, of the olive-wood Hermes and the snows of Samothrace. So Atta came to great honour among his own people, and his memory and his words were handed down to the generations. The song became a favourite island lay, and for centuries throughout the Aegean seafaring men sang it when they turned their prows to wild seas. Nay, it travelled farther, for you will find part of it stolen by Euripides and put in a chorus of the Andromache. There are echoes of it in some of the epigrams of the Anthology; and, though the old days have gone, the simple fisher-folk still sing snatches in their barbarous dialect. The Klephts used to make a catch of it at night round their fires in the hills, and only the other day I met a man in Scyros who had collected a dozen variants, and was publishing them in a dull book on island folklore.

In the centuries which followed the great fight, the sea fell away from the roots of the cliffs and left a mile of marshland. About fifty years ago a peasant, digging in a rice-field, found the cup which Atta bad given to Poseidon. There was much talk about the discovery, and scholars debated hotly about its origin. To-day it is in the Berlin Museum, and according to the new fashion in archaeology it is labelled "Minoan," and kept in the Cretan Section. But any one who looks carefully will see behind the rim a neat little carving of a dolphin; and I happen to know that that was the private badge of Atta's house.

ATTA'S SONG

(Roughly translated.)

I will sing of thee, Great Sea-Mother, Whose white arms gather Thy sons in the ending: And draw them homeward From far sad marches-- Wild lands in the sunset, Bitter shores of the morning-- Soothe them and guide them By shining pathways Homeward to thee.

All day I have striven in dark glens With parched throat and dim eyes, Where the red crags choke the stream And dank thickets hide the spear. I have spilled the blood of my foes And their wolves have torn my flanks. I am faint, O Mother, Faint and aweary. I have longed for thy cool winds And thy kind grey eyes And thy lover's arms.

At the even I came To a land of terrors, Of hot swamps where the feet mired And waters that flowerd red with blood There I strove with thousands, Wild-eyed and lost, As a lion among serpents. --But sudden before me I saw the flash Of the sweet wide waters That wash my homeland And mirror the stars of home. Then sang I for joy, For I knew the Preserver, Thee, the Uniter, The great Sea-Mother. Soon will the sweet light come, And the salt winds and the tides Will bear me home.

Far in the sunrise, Nestled in thy bosom, Lies my own green isle. Thither wilt thou bear me. To where, above the sea-cliffs, Stretch mild meadows, flower-decked, thyme-scented, Crisp with sea breezes. There my flocks feed On sunny uplands, Looking over thy waters To where the mount Saos Raises purl snows to God.

Hermes, guide of souls, I made thee a shrine in my orchard, And round thy olive-wood limbs The maidens twined Spring blossoms- Violet and helichryse And the pale wind flowers. Keep thou watch for me, For I am coming. Tell to my lady And to all my kinsfolk That I who have gone from them Tarry not long, but come swift o'er the sea-path, My feet light with joy, My eyes bright with longing. For little it matters Where a man may fall, If he fall by the sea-shore; The kind waters await him, The white arms are around him, And the wise Mother of Men Will carry him home.

I who sing Wait joyfully on the morning. Ten thousand beset me And their spears ache for my heart. They will crush me and grind me to mire, So that none will know the man that once was me. But at the first light I shall be gone, Singing, flitting, o'er the grey waters, Outward, homeward, To thee, the Preserver, Thee, the Uniter, Mother the Sea.

SPACE
IV

"Est impossibile? Certum est." -TERTULLIAN.

Leithen told me this story one evening in early September as we sat beside the pony track which gropes its way from Glenvalin up the Correi na Sidhe. I had arrived that afternoon from the south, while he had been taking an off-day from a week's stalking, so we had walked up the glen together after tea to get the news of the forest. A rifle was out on the Correi na Sidhe beat, and a thin spire of smoke had risen from the top of Sgurr Dearg to show that a stag had been killed at the burnhead. The lumpish hill pony with its deer-saddle had gone up the Correi in a gillie's charge while we followed at leisure, picking our way among the loose granite rocks and the patches of wet bogland. The track climbed high on one of the ridges of Sgurr Dearg, till it hung over a caldron of green glen with the Alt-na-Sidhe churning in its linn a thousand feet below. It was a breathless evening, I remember, with a pale-blue sky just clearing from the haze of the day. West-wind weather may make the North, even in September, no bad imitation of the Tropics, and I sincerely pitied the man who all these stifling hours had been toiling on the screes of Sgurr Dearg. By-and-by we sat down on a bank of heather, and idly watched the trough swimming at our feet. The clatter of the pony's hoofs grew fainter, the drone of bees had gone, even the midges seemed to have forgotten their calling. No place on earth can be so deathly still as a deer-forest early in the season before the stags have begun roaring, for there are no sheep with their homely noises, and only the rare croak of a raven breaks the silence. The hillside was far from sheer-one could have walked down with a little care-but something in the shape of the hollow and the remote gleam of white water gave it an extraordinary depth and space. There was a shimmer left from the day's heat, which invested bracken and rock and scree with a curious airy unreality. One could almost have believed that the eye had tricked the mind, that all was mirage, that five yards from the path the solid earth fell away into nothingness. I have a bad head, and instinctively I drew farther back into the heather. Leithen's eyes were looking vacantly before him.

"Did you ever know Hollond?" he asked.

Then he laughed shortly. "I don't know why I asked that, but somehow this place reminded me of Hollond. That glimmering hollow looks as if it were the beginning of eternity. It must be eerie to live with the feeling always on one."

Leithen seemed disinclined for further exercise. He lit a pipe and smoked quietly for a little. "Odd that you didn't know Hollond. You must have heard his name. I thought you amused yourself with metaphysics."

Then I remembered. There had been an erratic genius who had written some articles in Mind on that dreary subject, the mathematical conception of infinity. Men had praised them to me, but I confess I never quite understood their argument. "Wasn't he some sort of mathematical professor?" I asked.

"He was, and, in his own way, a tremendous swell. He wrote a book on Number which has translations in every European language. He is dead now, and the Royal Society founded a medal in his honour. But I wasn't thinking of that side of him."

It was the time and place for a story, for the pony would not be back for an hour. So I asked Leithen about the other side of Hollond which was recalled to him by Correi na Sidhe. He seemed a little unwilling to speak...

"I wonder if you will understand it. You ought to, of course, better than me, for you know something of philosophy. But it took me a long time to get the hang of it, and I can't give you any kind of explanation. He was my fag at Eton, and when I began to get on at the Bar I was able to advise him on one or two private matters, so that he rather fancied my legal ability. He came to me with his story because he had to tell someone, and he wouldn't trust a colleague. He said he didn't want a scientist to know, for scientists were either pledged to their own theories and wouldn't understand, or, if they understood, would get ahead of him in his researches. He wanted a lawyer, he said, who was accustomed to weighing evidence. That was good sense, for evidence must always be judged by the same laws, and I suppose in the long-run the most abstruse business comes down to a fairly simple deduction from certain data. Anyhow, that was the way he used to talk, and I listened to him, for I liked the man, and had an enormous respect for his brains. At Eton he sluiced down all the mathematics they could give him, and he was an astonishing swell at Cambridge. He was a simple fellow, too, and talked no more jargon than he could help. I used to climb with him in the Alps now and then, and you would never have guessed that he had any thoughts beyond getting up steep rocks.

"It was at Chamonix, I remember, that I first got a hint of the matter that was filling his mind. We had been taking an off-day, and were sitting in the hotel garden, watching the Aiguilles getting purple in the twilight. Chamonix always makes me choke a little-it is so crushed in by those great snow masses. I said something about it--said I liked the open spaces like the Gornegrat or the Bel Alp better. He asked me why: if it was the difference of the air, or merely the wider horizon? I said it was the sense of not being crowded, of living in an empty world. He repeated the word 'empty' and laughed.

"'By "empty" you mean,' he said,'where things don't knock up against you?'

I told him No. I mean just empty, void, nothing but blank aether.

"You don't knock up against things here, and the air is as good as you want. It can't be the lack of ordinary emptiness you feel."

"I agreed that the word needed explaining. 'I suppose it is mental restlessness,' I said. 'I like to feel that for a tremendous distance there is nothing round me. Why, I don't know. Some men are built the other way and have a terror of space.'

"He said that that was better. 'It is a personal fancy, and depends on your KNOWING that there is nothing between you and the top of the Dent Blanche. And you know because your eyes tell you there is nothing. Even if you were blind, you might have a sort of sense about adjacent matter. Blind men often have it. But in any case, whether got from instinct or sight, the KNOWLEDGE is what matters.'

"Hollond was embarking on a Socratic dialogue in which I could see little point. I told him so, and he laughed. "'I am not sure that I am very clear myself. But yes--there IS a point. Supposing you knew-not by sight or by instinct, but by sheer intellectual knowledge, as I know the truth of a mathematical proposition--that what we call empty space was full, crammed. Not with lumps of what we call matter like hills and houses, but with things as real--as real to the mind. Would you still feel crowded?'

"'No,' I said, 'I don't think so. It is only what we call matter that signifies. It would be just as well not to feel crowded by the other thing, for there would be no escape from it. But what are you getting at? Do you mean atoms or electric currents or what?'

"He said he wasn't thinking about that sort of thing, and began to talk of another subject.

"Next night, when we were pigging it at the Geant cabane, he started again on the same tack. He asked me how I accounted for the fact that animals could find their way back over great tracts of unknown country. I said I supposed it was the homing instinct.

"'Rubbish, man,' he said. 'That's only another name for the puzzle, not an explanation. There must be some reason for it. They must KNOW something that we cannot understand. Tie a cat in a bag and take it fifty miles by train and it will make its way home. That cat has some clue that we haven't.'

"I was tired and sleepy, and told him that I did not care a rush about the psychology of cats. But he was not to be snubbed, and went on talking.

"'How if Space is really full of things we cannot see and as yet do not know? How if all animals and some savages have a cell in their brain or a nerve which responds to the invisible world? How if all Space be full of these landmarks, not material in our sense, but quite real? A dog barks at nothing, a wild beast makes an aimless circuit. Why? Perhaps because Space is made up of corridors and alleys, ways to travel and things to shun? For all we know, to a greater intelligence than ours the top of Mont Blanc may be as crowded as Piccadilly Circus.'

"But at that point I fell asleep and left Hollond to repeat his questions to a guide who knew no English and a snoring porter.

"Six months later, one foggy January afternoon, Hollond rang me up at the Temple and proposed to come to see me that night after dinner. I thought he wanted to talk Alpine shop, but he turned up in Duke Street about nine with a kit-bag full of papers. He was an odd fellow to look at-- a yellowish face with the skin stretched tight on the cheek-bones, clean-shaven, a sharp chin which he kept poking forward, and deep-set, greyish eyes. He was a hard fellow, too, always in pretty good condition, which was remarkable considering how he slaved for nine months out of the twelve. He had a quiet, slow-spoken manner, but that night I saw that he was considerably excited.

"He said that he had come to me because we were old friends. He proposed to tell me a tremendous secret. 'I must get another mind to work on it or I'll go crazy. I don't want a scientist. I want a plain man.'

"Then he fixed me with a look like a tragic actor's. 'Do you remember that talk we had in August at Chamonix--about Space? I daresay you thought I was playing the fool. So I was in a sense, but I was feeling my way towards something which has been in my mind for ten years. Now I have got it, and you must hear about it. You may take my word that it's a pretty startling discovery.'

"I lit a pipe and told him to go ahead, warning him that I knew about as much science as the dustman.

"I am bound to say that it took me a long time to understand what he meant. He began by saying that everybody thought of Space as an 'empty homogeneous medium.' 'Never mind at present what the ultimate constituents of that medium are. We take it as a finished product, and we think of it as mere extension, something without any quality at all. That is the view of civilised man. You will find all the philosophers taking it for granted. Yes, but every living thing does not take that view. An animal, for instance. It feels a kind of quality in Space. It can find its way over new country, because it perceives certain landmarks, not necessarily material, but perceptible, or if you like intelligible. Take an Australian savage. He has the same power, and, I believe, for the same reason. He is conscious of intelligible landmarks.'

"'You mean what people call a sense of direction,' I put in.

"'Yes, but what in Heaven's name is a sense of direction? The phrase explains nothing. However incoherent the mind of the animal or the savage may be, it is there somewhere, working on some data. I've been all through the psychological and anthropological side of the business, and after you eliminate the clues from sight and hearing and smell and half-conscious memory there remains a solid lump of the inexplicable.'

"Hollond's eye had kindled, and he sat doubled up in his chair, dominating me with a finger.

"'Here, then is a power which man is civilising himself out of. Call it anything you like, but you must admit that it is a power. Don't you see that it is a perception of another kind of reality that we are leaving behind us? ', Well, you know the way nature works. The wheel comes full circle, and what we think we have lost we regain in a higher form. So for a long time I have been wondering whether the civilised mind could not recreate for itself this lost gift, the gift of seeing the quality of Space. I mean that I wondered whether the scientific modern brain could not get to the stage of realising that Space is not an empty homogeneous medium, but full of intricate differences, intelligible and real, though not with our common reality.'

"I found all this very puzzling and he had to repeat it several times before I got a glimpse of what he was talking about.

"'I've wondered for a long time he went on 'but now quite suddenly, I have begun to know.' He stopped and asked me abruptly if I knew much about mathematics.

"'It's a pity,' he said,'but the main point is not technical, though I wish you could appreciate the beauty of some of my proofs. Then he began to tell me about his last six months' work. I should have mentioned that he was a brilliant physicist besides other things. All Hollond's tastes were on the borderlands of sciences, where mathematics fades into metaphysics and physics merges in the abstrusest kind of mathematics. Well, it seems he had been working for years at the ultimate problem of matter, and especially of that rarefied matter we call aether or space. I forget what his view was-atoms or molecules or electric waves. If he ever told me I have forgotten, but I'm not certain that I ever knew. However, the point was that these ultimate constituents were dynamic and mobile, not a mere passive medium but a medium in constant movement and change. He claimed to have discovered--by ordinary inductive experiment--that the constituents of aether possessed certain functions, and moved in certain figures obedient to certain mathematical laws. Space, I gathered, was perpetually 'forming fours' in some fancy way.

"Here he left his physics and became the mathematician. Among his mathematical discoveries had been certain curves or figures or something whose behaviour involved a new dimension. I gathered that this wasn't the ordinary Fourth Dimension that people talk of, but that fourth-dimensional inwardness or involution was part of it. The explanation lay in the pile of manuscripts he left with me, but though I tried honestly I couldn't get the hang of it. My mathematics stopped with desperate finality just as he got into his subject.

"His point was that the constituents of Space moved according to these new mathematical figures of his. They were always changing, but the principles of their change were as fixed as the law of gravitation. Therefore, if you once grasped these principles you knew the contents of the void. What do you make of that?"

I said that it seemed to me a reasonable enough argument, but that it got one very little way forward. "A man," I said, "might know the contents of Space and the laws of their arrangement and yet be unable to see anything more than his fellows. It is a purely academic knowledge. His mind knows it as the result of many deductions, but his senses perceive nothing."

Leithen laughed. "Just what I said to Hollond. He asked the opinion of my legal mind. I said I could not pronounce on his argument but that I could point out that he had established no trait d'union between the intellect which understood and the senses which perceived. It was like a blind man with immense knowledge but no eyes, and therefore no peg to hang his knowledge on and make it useful. He had not explained his savage or his cat. 'Hang it, man,' I said, 'before you can appreciate the existence of your Spacial forms you have to go through elaborate experiments and deductions. You can't be doing that every minute. Therefore you don't get any nearer to the USE of the sense you say that man once possessed, though you can explain it a bit.'"

"What did he say?" I asked.

"The funny thing was that he never seemed to see my difficulty. When I kept bringing him back to it he shied off with a new wild theory of perception. He argued that the mind can live in a world of realities without any sensuous stimulus to connect them with the world of our ordinary life. Of course that wasn't my point. I supposed that this world of Space was real enough to him, but I wanted to know how he got there. He never answered me. He was the typical Cambridge man, you know-- dogmatic about uncertainties, but curiously diffident about the obvious. He laboured to get me to understand the notion of his mathematical forms, which I was quite willing to take on trust from him. Some queer things he said, too. He took our feeling about Left and Right as an example of our instinct for the quality of Space. But when I objected that Left and Right varied with each object, and only existed in connection with some definite material thing, he said that that was exactly what he meant. It was an example of the mobility of the Spacial forms. Do you see any sense in that?"

I shook my head. It seemed to me pure craziness.

"And then he tried to show me what he called the 'involution of Space,' by taking two points on a piece of paper. The points were a foot away when the paper was flat, they coincided when it was doubled up. He said that there were no gaps between the figures, for the medium was continuous, and he took as an illustration the loops on a cord. You are to think of a cord always looping and unlooping itself according to certain mathematical laws. Oh, I tell you, I gave up trying to follow him. And he was so desperately in earnest all the time. By his account Space was a sort of mathematical pandemonium."

Leithen stopped to refill his pipe, and I mused upon the ironic fate which had compelled a mathematical genius to make his sole confidant of a philistine lawyer, and induced that lawyer to repeat it confusedly to an ignoramus at twilight on a Scotch hill. As told by Leithen it was a very halting tale.

"But there was one thing I could see very clearly," Leithen went on, "and that was Hollond's own case. This crowded world of Space was perfectly real to him. How he had got to it I do not know. Perhaps his mind, dwelling constantly on the problem, had unsealed some atrophied cell and restored the old instinct. Anyhow, he was living his daily life with a foot in each world.

"He often came to see me, and after the first hectic discussions he didn't talk much. There was no noticeable change in him--a little more abstracted perhaps. He would walk in the street or come into a room with a quick look round him, and sometimes for no earthly reason he would swerve. Did you ever watch a cat crossing a room? It sidles along by the furniture and walks over an open space of carpet as if it were picking its way among obstacles. Well, Hollond behaved like that, but he had always been counted a little odd, and nobody noticed it but me.

"I knew better than to chaff him, and had stopped argument, so there wasn't much to be said. But sometimes he would give me news about his experiences. The whole thing was perfectly clear and scientific and above board, and nothing creepy about it. You know how I hate the washy supernatural stuff they give us nowadays. Hollond was well and fit, with an appetite like a hunter. But as he talked, sometimes--well, you know I haven't much in the way of nerves or imagination--but I used to get a little eerie. Used to feel the solid earth dissolving round me. It was the opposite of vertigo, if you understand me--a sense of airy realities crowding in on you-crowding the mind, that is, not the body.

"I gathered from Hollond that he was always conscious of corridors and halls and alleys in Space, shifting, but shifting according to inexorable laws. I never could get quite clear as to what this consciousness was like. When I asked he used to look puzzled and worried and helpless. I made out from him that one landmark involved a sequence, and once given a bearing from an object you could keep the direction without a mistake. He told me he could easily, if he wanted, go in a dirigible from the top of Mont Blanc to the top of Snowdon in the thickest fog and without a compass, if he were given the proper angle to start from. I confess I didn't follow that myself. Material objects had nothing to do with the Spacial forms, for a table or a bed in our world might be placed across a corridor of Space. The forms played their game independent of our kind of reality. But the worst of it was, that if you kept your mind too much in one world you were apt to forget about the other and Hollond was always barking his shins on stones and chairs and things.

"He told me all this quite simply and frankly. Remember his mind and no other part of him lived in his new world. He said it gave him an odd sense of detachment to sit in a room among people, and to know that nothing there but himself had any relation at all to the infinite strange world of Space that flowed around them. He would listen, he said, to a great man talking, with one eye on the cat on the rug, thinking to himself how much more the cat knew than the man."

"How long was it before he went mad?" I asked.

It was a foolish question, and made Leithen cross. "He never went mad in your sense. My dear fellow, you're very much wrong if you think there was anything pathological about him--then. The man was brilliantly sane. His mind was as keen is a keen sword. I couldn't understand him, but I could judge of his sanity right enough."

I asked if it made him happy or miserable.

"At first I think it made him uncomfortable. He was restless because he knew too much and too little. The unknown pressed in on his mind as bad air weighs on the lungs. Then it lightened and he accepted the new world in the same sober practical way that he took other things. I think that the free exercise of his mind in a pure medium gave him a feeling of extraordinary power and ease. His eyes used to sparkle when he talked. And another odd thing he told me. He was a keen rockclimber, but, curiously enough, he had never a very good head. Dizzy heights always worried him, though he managed to keep hold on himself. But now all that had gone. The sense of the fulness of Space made him as happy--happier I believe--with his legs dangling into eternity, as sitting before his own study fire.

"I remember saying that it was all rather like the mediaeval wizards who made their spells by means of numbers and figures.

"He caught me up at once. 'Not numbers,' he said. "Number has no place in Nature. It is an invention of the human mind to atone for a bad memory. But figures are a different matter. All the mysteries of the world are in them, and the old magicians knew that at least, if they knew no more.'

"He had only one grievance. He complained that it was terribly lonely. 'It is the Desolation,' he would quote, 'spoken of by Daniel the prophet.' He would spend hours travelling those eerie shifting corridors of Space with no hint of another human soul. How could there be? It was a world of pure reason, where human personality had no place. What puzzled me was why he should feel the absence of this. One wouldn't you know, in an intricate problem of geometry or a game of chess. I asked him, but he didn't understand the question. I puzzled over it a good deal, for it seemed to me that if Hollond felt lonely, there must be more in this world of his than we imagined. I began to wonder if there was any truth in fads like psychical research. Also, I was not so sure that he was as normal as I had thought: it looked as if his nerves might be going bad.

"Oddly enough, Hollond was getting on the same track himself. He had discovered, so he said, that in sleep everybody now and then lived in this new world of his. You know how one dreams of triangular railway platforms with trains running simultaneously down all three sides and not colliding. Well, this sort of cantrip was 'common form,' as we say at the Bar, in Hollond's Space, and he was very curious about the why and wherefore of Sleep. He began to haunt psychological laboratories, where they experiment with the charwoman and the odd man, and he used to go up to Cambridge for seances. It was a foreign atmosphere to him, and I don't think he was very happy in it. He found so many charlatans that he used to get angry, and declare he would be better employed at Mother's Meetings!"

From far up the Glen came the sound of the pony's hoofs. The stag had been loaded up and the gillies were returning. Leithen looked at his watch. "We'd better wait and see the beast," he said.

"... Well, nothing happened for more than a year. Then one evening in May he burst into my rooms in high excitement. You understand quite clearly that there was no suspicion of horror or fright or anything unpleasant about this world he had discovered. It was simply a series of interesting and difficult problems. All this time Hollond had been rather extra well and cheery. But when he came in I thought I noticed a different look in his eyes, something puzzled and diffident and apprehensive .

"'There's a queer performance going on in the other world,' he said. 'It's unbelievable. I never dreamed of such a thing. I-- I don't quite know how to put it, and I don't know how to explain it, but--but I am becoming aware that there are other beings-- other minds--moving in Space besides mine.'

"I suppose I ought to have realised then that things were beginning to go wrong. But it was very difficult, he was so rational and anxious to make it all clear. I asked him how he knew. 'There could, of course, on his own showing be no CHANGE in that world, for the forms of Space moved and existed under inexorable laws. He said he found his own mind failing him at points. There would come over him a sense of fear-- intellectual fear--and weakness, a sense of something else, quite alien to Space, thwarting him. Of course he could only describe his impressions very lamely, for they were purely of the mind, and he had no material peg to hang them on, so that I could realise them. But the gist of it was that he had been gradually becoming conscious of what he called 'Presences' in his world. They had no effect on Space--did not leave footprints in its corridors, for instance--but they affected his mind. There was some mysterious contact established between him and them. I asked him if the affection was unpleasant and he said 'No, not exactly.' But I could see a hint of fear in his eyes.

"Think of it. Try to realise what intellectual fear is. I can't, but it is conceivable. To you and me fear implies pain to ourselves or some other, and such pain is always in the last resort pain of the flesh. Consider it carefully and you will see that it is so. But imagine fear so sublimated and transmuted as to be the tension of pure spirit. I can't realise it, but I think it possible. I don't pretend to understand how Hollond got to know about these Presences. But there was no doubt about the fact. He was positive, and he wasn't in the least mad--not in our sense. In that very month he published his book on Number, and gave a German professor who attacked it a most tremendous public trouncing.

"I know what you are going to say,--that the fancy was a weakening of the mind from within. I admit I should have thought of that but he looked so confoundedly sane and able that it seemed ridiculous. He kept asking me my opinion, as a lawyer, on the facts he offered. It was the oddest case ever put before me, but I did my best for him. I dropped all my own views of sense and nonsense. I told him that, taking all that he had told me as fact, the Prescences might be either ordinary minds traversing Space in sleep; or minds such as his which had independently captured the sense of Space's quality; or, finally, the spirits of just men made perfect, behaving as psychical researchers think they do. It was a ridiculous task to set a prosaic man, and I wasn't quite serious. But Holland was serious enough.

"He admitted that all three explanations were conceivable, but he was very doubtful about the first. The projection of the spirit into Space during sleep, he thought, was a faint and feeble thing, and these were powerful Presences. With the second and the third he was rather impressed. I suppose I should have seen what was happening and tried to stop it; at least, looking back that seems to have been my duty. But it was difficult to think that anything was wrong with Hollond; indeed the odd thing is that all this time the idea of madness never entered my head. I rather backed him up. Somehow the thing took my fancy, though I thought it moonshine at the bottom of my heart. I enlarged on the pioneering before him. 'Think,' I told him, 'what may be waiting for you.

You may discover the meaning of Spirit. You may open up a new world, as rich as the old one, but imperishable. You may prove to mankind their immortality and deliver them for ever from the fear of death. Why, man, you are picking at the lock of all the world's mysteries.'

"But Hollond did not cheer up. He seemed strangely languid and dispirited. 'That is all true enough,' he said,'if you are right, if your alternatives are exhaustive. But suppose they are something else, something .... What that 'something' might be he had apparently no idea, and very soon he went away.

"He said another thing before he left. We asked me if I ever read poetry, and I said, not often. Nor did he: but he had picked up a little book somewhere and found a man who knew about the Presences. I think his name was Traherne, one of the seventeenth-century fellows. He quoted a verse which stuck to my fly-paper memory. It ran something like

'Within the region of the air, Compassed about with Heavens fair, Great tracts of lands there may be found, Where many numerous hosts, In those far distant coasts, For other great and glorious ends Inhabit, my yet unknown friends.'

Hollond was positive he did not mean angels or anything of the sort. I told him that Traherne evidently took a cheerful view of them. He admitted that, but added: 'He had religion, you see. He believed that everything was for the best. I am not a man of faith, and can only take comfort from what I understand. I'm in the dark, I tell you...'

"Next week I was busy with the Chilian Arbitration case, and saw nobody for a couple of months. Then one evening I ran against Hollond on the Embankment, and thought him looking horribly ill. He walked back with me to my rooms, and hardly uttered one word all the way. I gave him a stiff whisky-and-soda, which he gulped down absent-mindedly. There was that strained, hunted look in his eyes that you see in a frightened animal's. He was always lean, but now he had fallen away to skin and bone.

"'I can't stay long,' he told me, 'for I'm off to the Alps to-morrow and I have a lot to do.' Before then he used to plunge readily into his story, but now he seemed shy about beginning. Indeed I had to ask him a question.

"'Things are difficult,' he said hesitatingly, and rather distressing. Do you know, Leithen, I think you were wrong about--about what I spoke to you of. You said there must be one of three explanations. I am beginning to think that there is a fourth.

"He stopped for a second or two, then suddenly leaned forward and gripped my knee so fiercely that I cried out. 'That world is the Desolation,' he said in a choking voice, 'and perhaps I am getting near the Abomination of the Desolation that the old prophet spoke of. I tell you, man, I am on the edge of a terror, a terror,' he almost screamed, 'that no mortal can think of and live.'

You can imagine that I was considerably startled. It was lightning out of a clear sky. How the devil could one associate horror with mathematics? I don't see it yet... At any rate, I-- You may he sure I cursed my folly for ever pretending to take him seriously. The only way would have been to have laughed him out of it at the start. And yet I couldn't, you know--it was too real and reasonable. Anyhow, I tried a firm tone now, and told him the whole thing was arrant raving bosh. I bade him be a man and pull himself together. I made him dine with me, and took him home, and got him into a better state of mind before he went to bed. Next morning I saw him off at Charing Cross, very haggard still, but better. He promised to write to me pretty often...."

The pony, with a great eleven-pointer lurching athwart its back, was abreast of us, and from the autumn mist came the sound of soft Highland voices. Leithen and I got up to go, when we heard that the rifle had made direct for the Lodge by a short cut past the Sanctuary. In the wake of the gillies we descended the Correi road into a glen all swimming with dim purple shadows. The pony minced and boggled; the stag's antlers stood out sharp on the rise against a patch of sky, looking like a skeleton tree. Then we dropped into a covert of birches and emerged on the white glen highway.

Leithen's story had bored and puzzled me at the start, but now it had somehow gripped my fancy. Space a domain of endless corridors and Presences moving in them! The world was not quite the same as an hour ago. It was the hour, as the French say, "between dog and wolf," when the mind is disposed to marvels. I thought of my stalking on the morrow, and was miserably conscious that I would miss my stag. Those airy forms would get in the way. Confound Leithen and his yarns!

"I want to hear the end of your story," I told him, as the lights of the Lodge showed half a mile distant.

"The end was a tragedy," he said slowly. "I don't much care to talk about it. But how was I to know? I couldn't see the nerve going. You see I couldn't believe it was all nonsense. If I could I might have seen. But I still think there was something in it--up to a point. Oh, I agree he went mad in the end. It is the only explanation. Something must have snapped in that fine brain, and he saw the little bit more which we call madness. Thank God, you and I are prosaic fellows...

"I was going out to Chamonix myself a week later. But before I started I got a post-card from Hollond, the only word from him. He had printed my name and address, and on the other side had scribbled six words--' I know at last--God's mercy.--H.G.H' The handwriting was like a sick man of ninety. I knew that things must be pretty bad with my friend.

"I got to Chamonix in time for his funeral. An ordinary climbing accident--you probably read about it in the papers. The Press talked about the toll which the Alps took from intellectuals--the usual rot. There was an inquiry, but the facts were quite simple. The body was only recognised by the clothes. He had fallen several thousand feet.

"It seems that he had climbed for a few days with one of the Kronigs and Dupont, and they had done some hair-raising things on the Aiguilles. Dupont told me that they had found a new route up the Montanvert side of the Charmoz. He said that Hollond climbed like a 'diable fou' and if you know Dupont's standard of madness you will see that the pace must have been pretty hot. 'But monsieur was sick,' he added; 'his eyes were not good. And I and Franz, we were grieved for him and a little afraid. We were glad when he left us.'

"He dismissed the guides two days before his death. The next day he spent in the hotel, getting his affairs straight. He left everything in perfect order, but not a line to a soul, not even to his sister. The following day he set out alone about three in the morning for the Grepon. He took the road up the Nantillons glacier to the Col, and then he must have climbed the Mummery crack by himself. After that he left the ordinary route and tried a new traverse across the Mer de Glace face. Somewhere near the top he fell, and next day a party going to the Dent du Requin found him on the rocks thousands of feet below.

"He had slipped in attempting the most foolhardy course on earth, and there was a lot of talk about the dangers of guideless climbing. But I guessed the truth, and I am sure Dupont knew, though he held his tongue...."

We were now on the gravel of the drive, and I was feeling better. The thought of dinner warmed my heart and drove out the eeriness of the twilight glen. The hour between dog and wolf was passing. After all, there was a gross and jolly earth at hand for wise men who had a mind to comfort.

Leithen, I saw, did not share my mood. He looked glum and puzzled, as if his tale had aroused grim memories. He finished it at the Lodge door.

"... For, of course, he had gone out that day to die. He had seen the something more, the little bit too much, which plucks a man from his moorings. He had gone so far into the land of pure spirit that he must needs go further and shed the fleshly envelope that cumbered him. God send that he found rest! I believe that he chose the steepest cliff in the Alps for a purpose. He wanted to be unrecognisable. He was a brave man and a good citizen. I think he hoped that those who found him might not see the look in his eyes."

STOCKS AND STONES

[The Chief Topaiwari replieth to Sir Walter Raleigh who upbraideth him for idol worship]

My gods, you say, are idols dumb, Which men have wrought from wood or clay, Carven with chisel, shaped with thumb, A morning's task, an evening's play. You bid me turn my face on high Where the blue heaven the sun enthrones, And serve a viewless deity, Nor make my bow to stocks and stones.

My lord, I am not skilled in wit Nor wise in priestcraft, but I know That fear to man is spur and bit To jog and curb his fancies' flow. He fears and loves, for love and awe In mortal souls may well unite To fashion forth the perfect law Where Duty takes to wife Delight.

But on each man one Fear awaits And chills his marrow like the dead.-- He cannot worship what he hates Or make a god of naked Dread. The homeless winds that twist and race, The heights of cloud that veer and roll, The unplumb'd Abyss, the drift of Space-- These are the fears that drain the soul.

Ye dauntless ones from out the sea Fear nought. Perchance your gods are strong To rule the air where grim things be, And quell the deeps with all their throng. For me, I dread not fire nor steel, Nor aught that walks in open light, But fend me from the endless Wheel, The voids of Space, the gulfs of Night.

Wherefore my brittle gods I make Of friendly clay and kindly stone,-- Wrought with my hands, to serve or break, From crown to toe my work, my own. My eyes can see, my nose can smell, My fingers touch their painted face, They weave their little homely spell To warm me from the cold of Space.

My gods are wrought of common stuff For human joys and mortal tears; Weakly, perchance, yet staunch enough To build a barrier 'gainst my fears, Where, lowly but secure, I wait And hear without the strange winds blow.-- I cannot worship what I hate, Or serve a god I dare not know.

STREAMS OF WATER IN THE SOUTH
V

" As streams of water in the south, Our bondage, Lord, recall. -PSALM cxxvi. (Scots Metrical Version).

It was at the ford of the Clachlands Water in a tempestuous August, that I, an idle boy, first learned the hardships of the Lammas droving. The shepherd of the Redswirehead, my very good friend, and his three shaggy dogs, were working for their lives in an angry water. The path behind was thronged with scores of sheep bound for the Gledsmuir market, and beyond it was possible to discern through the mist the few dripping dozen which had made the passage. Between raged yards of brown foam coming down from murky hills, and the air echoed with the yelp of dogs and the perplexed cursing of men.

Before I knew I was helping in the task, with water lipping round my waist and my arms filled with a terrified sheep. It was no light task, for though the water was no more than three feet deep it was swift and strong, and a kicking hogg is a sore burden. But this was the only road; the stream might rise higher at any moment; and somehow or other those bleating flocks had to be transferred to their fellows beyond. There were six men at the labour, six men and myself and all were cross and wearied and heavy with water.

I made my passages side by side with my friend the shepherd, and thereby felt much elated. This was a man who had dwelt all his days in the wilds and was familiar with torrents as with his own doorstep. Now and then a swimming dog would bark feebly as he was washed against us, and flatter his fool's heart that he was aiding the work. And so we wrought on, till by midday I was dead-beat, and could scarce stagger through the surf, while all the men had the same gasping faces. I saw the shepherd look with longing eye up the long green valley, and mutter disconsolately in his beard.

"Is the water rising?" I asked.

"It's no rising," said he, " but I likena the look o' yon big black clud upon Cairncraw. I doubt there's been a shoor up the muirs, and a shoor there means twae mair feet o' water in the Clachlands. God help Sandy Jamieson's lambs, if there is."

"How many are left?" I asked.

"Three, fower,--no abune a score and a half," said he, running his eye over the lessened flocks. "I maun try to tak twae at a time." So for ten minutes he struggled with a double burden, and panted painfully at each return. Then with a sudden swift look up-stream he broke off and stood up. "Get ower the water, every yin o' ye, and leave the sheep," he said, and to my wonder every man of the five obeyed his word.

And then I saw the reason of his command, for with a sudden swift leap forward the Clachlands rose, and flooded up to where I stood an instant before high and dry.

"It's come," said the shepherd in a tone of fate, "and there's fifteen no ower yet, and Lord kens how they'll dae't. They'll hae to gang roond by Gledsmuir Brig, and that's twenty mile o' a differ. 'Deed, it's no like that Sandy Jamieson will get a guid price the morn for sic sair forfochen beasts."

Then with firmly gripped staff he marched stoutly into the tide till it ran hissing below his armpits. "I could dae't alone," he cried, "but no wi' a burden. For, losh, if ye slippit, ye'd be in the Manor Pool afore ye could draw breath."

And so we waited with the great white droves and five angry men beyond, and the path blocked by a surging flood. For half an hour we waited, holding anxious consultation across the stream, when to us thus busied there entered a newcomer, a helper from the ends of the earth.

He was a man of something over middle size, but with a stoop forward that shortened him to something beneath it. His dress was ragged homespun, the cast-off clothes of some sportsman, and in his arms he bore a bundle of sticks and heather-roots which marked his calling. I knew him for a tramp who long had wandered in the place, but I could not account for the whole-voiced shout of greeting which met him as he stalked down the path. He lifted his eyes and looked solemnly and long at the scene. Then something of delight came into his eye, his face relaxed, and flinging down his burden he stripped his coat and came toward us.

"Come on, Yeddie, ye're sair needed," said the shepherd, and I watched with amazement this grizzled, crooked man seize a sheep by the fleece and drag it to the water. Then he was in the midst, stepping warily, now up, now down the channel, but always nearing the farther bank. At last with a final struggle he landed his charge, and turned to journey back. Fifteen times did he cross that water, and at the end his mean figure had wholly changed. For now he was straighter and stronger, his eye flashed, and his voice, as he cried out to the drovers, had in it a tone of command. I marvelled at the transformation; and when at length he had donned once more his ragged coat and shouldered his bundle, I asked the shepherd his name.

"They ca' him Adam Logan," said my friend, his face still bright with excitement, "but maist folk ca' him 'Streams o' Water.'"

"Ay," said I, "and why 'Streams of Water'?"

"Juist for the reason ye see," said he.

Now I knew the shepherd's way, and I held my peace, for it was clear that his mind was revolving other matters, concerned most probably with the high subject of the morrow's prices. But in a little, as we crossed the moor toward his dwelling, his thoughts relaxed and he remembered my question. So he answered me thus:

"Oh, ay; as ye were sayin', he's a queer man Yeddie-aye been; guid kens whaur he cam frae first, for he's been trampin' the countryside since ever I mind, and that's no yesterday. He maun be sixty year, and yet he's as fresh as ever. If onything, he's a thocht dafter in his ongaein's, mair silent-like. But ye'll hae heard tell o' him afore?" I owned ignorance.

"Tut," said he, "ye ken nocht. But Yeddie had aye a queer crakin' for waters. He never gangs on the road. Wi' him it's juist up yae glen and doon anither and aye keepin' by the burn-side. He kens every water i' the warld, every bit sheuch and burnie frae Gallowa' to Berwick. And then he kens the way o' spates the best I ever seen, and I've heard tell o' him fordin' waters when nae ither thing could leeve i' them. He can weyse and wark his road sae cunnin'ly on the stanes that the roughest flood, if it's no juist fair ower his heid, canna upset him. Mony a sheep has he saved to me, and it's mony a guid drove wad never hae won to Gledsmuir market but for Yeddie."

I listened with a boy's interest in any romantic narration. Somehow, the strange figure wrestling in the brown stream took fast hold on my mind, and I asked the shepherd for further tales.

"There's little mair to tell," he said, "for a gangrel life is nane o' the liveliest. But d'ye ken the langnebbit hill that cocks its tap abune the Clachlands heid? Weel, he's got a wee bit o' grund on the tap frae the Yerl, and there he's howkit a grave for himsel'. He's sworn me and twae-three ithers to bury him there, wherever he may dee. It's a queer fancy in the auld dotterel."

So the shepherd talked, and as at evening we stood by his door we saw a figure moving into the gathering shadows. I knew it at once, and did not need my friend's "There gangs 'Streams o' Water'" to recognise it. Something wild and pathetic in the old man's face haunted me like a dream, and as the dusk swallowed him up, he seemed like some old Druid recalled of the gods to his ancient habitation of the moors.

II

Two years passed, and April came with her suns and rains and again the waters brimmed full in the valleys. Under the clear, shining sky the lambing went on, and the faint bleat of sheep brooded on the hills. In a land of young heather and green upland meads, of faint odours of moor-burn, and hill-tops falling in clear ridges to the sky-line, the veriest St. Anthony would not abide indoors; so I flung all else to the winds and went a-fishing.

At the first pool on the Callowa, where the great flood sweeps nobly round a ragged shoulder of hill, and spreads into broad deeps beneath a tangle of birches, I began my toils. The turf was still wet with dew and the young leaves gleamed in the glow of morning. Far up the stream rose the grim hills which hem the mosses and tarns of that tableland, whence flow the greater waters of the countryside. An ineffable freshness, as of the morning alike of the day and the seasons, filled the clear hill-air, and the remote peaks gave the needed touch of intangible romance.

But as I fished I came on a man sitting in a green dell, busy at the making of brooms. I knew his face and dress, for who could forget such eclectic raggedness?--and I remembered that day two years before when he first hobbled into my ken. Now, as I saw him there, I was captivated by the nameless mystery of his appearance. There was something startling to one accustomed to the lack-lustre gaze of town-bred folk, in the sight of an eye as keen and wild as a hawk's from sheer solitude and lonely travelling. He was so bent and scarred with weather that he seemed as much a part of that woodland place as the birks themselves, and the noise of his labours did not startle the birds that hopped on the branches.

Little by little I won his acquaintance--by a chance reminiscence, a single tale, the mention of a friend. Then he made me free of his knowledge, and my fishing fared well that day. He dragged me up little streams to sequestered pools, where I had astonishing success; and then back to some great swirl in the Callowa where he had seen monstrous takes. And all the while he delighted me with his talk, of men and things, of weather and place, pitched high in his thin, old voice, and garnished with many tones of lingering sentiment. He spoke in a broad, slow Scots, with so quaint a lilt in his speech that one seemed to be in an elder time among people of a quieter life and a quainter kindliness.

Then by chance I asked him of a burn of which I had heard, and how it might he reached. I shall never forget the tone of his answer as his face grew eager and he poured forth his knowledge.

"Ye'll gang up the Knowe Burn, which comes down into the Cauldshaw. It's a wee tricklin' thing, trowin' in and out o' pools i' the rock, and comin' doun out o' the side o' Caerfraun. Yince a merrymaiden bided there, I've heard folks say, and used to win the sheep frae the Cauldshaw herd, and bile them i' the muckle pool below the fa'. They say that there's a road to the ill Place there, and when the Deil likit he sent up the lowe and garred the water faem and fizzle like an auld kettle. But if ye're gaun to the Colm Burn ye maun haud atower the rig o' the hill frae the Knowe heid, and ye'll come to it wimplin' among green brae faces. It's a bonny bit, rale lonesome, but awfu' bonny, and there's mony braw trout in its siller flow."

Then I remembered all I had heard of the old man's craze, and I humoured him. "It's a fine countryside for burns," I said.

"Ye may say that," said he gladly, "a weel-watered land. But a' this braw south country is the same. I've traivelled frae the Yeavering Hill in the Cheviots to the Caldons in Galloway, and it's a' the same. When I was young, I've seen me gang north to the Hielands and doun to the English lawlands, but now that I'm gettin' auld I maun bide i' the yae place. There's no a burn in the South I dinna ken, and I never cam to the water I couldna ford."

"No?" said I. "I've seen you at the ford o' Clachlands in the Lammas floods."

"Often I've been there," he went on, speaking like one calling up vague memories. "Yince, when Tam Rorison was drooned, honest man. Yince again, when the brigs were ta'en awa', and the Black House o' Clachlands had nae bread for a week. But oh, Clachlands is a bit easy water. But I've seen the muckle Aller come roarin' sae high that it washed awa' a sheepfold that stood weel up on the hill. And I've seen this verra burn, this bonny clear Callowa, lyin' like a loch for miles i' the haugh. But I never heeds a spate, for if a man just kens the way o't it's a canny, hairmless thing. I couldna wish to dee better than just be happit i' the waters o' my ain countryside, when my legs fail and I'm ower auld for the trampin'."

Something in that queer figure in the setting of the hills struck a note of curious pathos. And towards evening as we returned down the glen the note grew keener. A spring sunset of gold and crimson flamed in our backs and turned the clear pools to fire. Far off down the vale the plains and the sea gleamed half in shadow. Somehow in the fragrance and colour and the delectable crooning of the stream, the fantastic and the dim seemed tangible and present, and high sentiment revelled for once in my prosaic heart.

And still more in the breast of my companion. He stopped and sniffed the evening air, as he looked far over hill and dale and then back to the great hills above us. "Yen's Crappel, and Caerdon, and the Laigh Law," he said, lingering with relish over each name, "and the Gled comes doun atween them. I haena been there for a twalmonth, and I maun hae anither glisk o't, for it's a braw place." And then some bitter thought seemed to seize him, and his mouth twitched. "I'm an auld man," he cried, " and I canna see ye a' again. There's burns and mair burns in the high hills that I'll never win to." Then he remembered my presence, and stopped. "Ye maunna mind me," he said huskily, " but the sicht o' a' thae lang blue hills makes me daft, now that I've faun i' the vale o' years. Yince I was young and could get where I wantit, but now I am auld and maun bide i' the same bit. And I'm aye thinkin' o' the waters I've been to, and the green heichs and howes and the linns that I canna win to again. I maun e'en be content wi' the Callowa, which is as guid as the best."

And then I left him, wandering down by the streamside and telling his crazy meditations to himself.

III

A space of years elapsed ere I met him, for fate had carried me far from the upland valleys. But once again I was afoot on the white moor-roads; and, as I swung along one autumn afternoon up the path which leads from the Glen of Callowa to the Gled, I saw a figure before me which I knew for my friend. When I overtook him, his appearance puzzled and troubled me. Age seemed to have come on him at a bound, and in the tottering figure and the stoop of weakness I had difficulty in recognising the hardy frame of the man as I had known him. Something, too, had come over his face. His brow was clouded, and the tan of weather stood out hard and cruel on a blanched cheek. His eye seemed both wilder and sicklier, and for the first time I saw him with none of the appurtenances of his trade. He greeted me feebly and dully, and showed little wish to speak. He walked with slow, uncertain step, and his breath laboured with a new panting. Every now and then he would look at me sidewise, and in his feverish glance I could detect none of the free kindliness of old. The man was ill in body and mind.

I asked him how he had done since I saw him last.

"It's an ill world now," he said in a slow, querulous voice.

"There's nae need for honest men, and nae leevin'. Folk dinna heed me ava now. They dinna buy my besoms, they winna let me bide a nicht in their byres, and they're no like the kind canty folk in the auld times. And a' the countryside is changin'. Doun by Goldieslaw they're makkin' a dam for takin' water to the toun, and they're thinkin' o' daein' the like wi' the Callowa. Guid help us, can they no let the works o' God alane? Is there no room for them in the dirty lawlands that they maun file the hills wi' their biggins?"

I conceived dimly that the cause of his wrath was a scheme for waterworks at the border of the uplands, but I had less concern for this than his strangely feeble health.

"You are looking ill," I said. "What has come over you?"

"Oh, I canna last for aye," he said mournfully. "My auld body's about dune. I've warkit it ower sair when I had it, and it's gaun to fail on my hands. Sleepin' out o' wat nichts and gangin' lang wantin' meat are no the best ways for a long life"; and he smiled the ghost of a smile.

And then he fell to wild telling of the ruin of the place and the hardness of the people, and I saw that want and bare living had gone far to loosen his wits. I knew the countryside, and I recognised that change was only in his mind. And a great pity seized me for this lonely figure toiling on in the bitterness of regret. I tried to comfort him, but my words were useless, for he took no heed of me; with bent head and faltering step he mumbled his sorrows to himself.

Then of a sudden we came to the crest of the ridge where the road dips from the hill-top to the sheltered valley. Sheer from the heather ran the white streak till it lost itself among the reddening rowans and the yellow birks of the wood. The land was rich in autumn colour, and the shining waters dipped and fell through a pageant of russet and gold. And all around hills huddled in silent spaces, long brown moors crowned with cairns, or steep fortresses of rock and shingle rising to foreheads of steel-like grey. The autumn blue faded in the far sky-line to white, and lent distance to the farther peaks. The hush of the wilderness, which is far different from the hush of death, brooded over the scene, and like faint music came the sound of a distant scytheswing, and the tinkling whisper which is the flow of a hundred streams.

I am an old connoisseur in the beauties of the uplands, but I held my breath at the sight. And when I glanced at my companion, he, too, had raised his head, and stood with wide nostrils and gleaming eye revelling in this glimpse of Arcady. Then he found his voice, and the weakness and craziness seemed for one moment to leave him.

"It's my ain land," he cried, "and I'll never leave it. D'ye see yon broun hill wi' the lang cairn?" and he gripped my arm fiercely and directed my gaze. "Yon's my bit. I howkit it richt on the verra tap, and ilka year I gang there to make it neat and ordlerly. I've trystit wi' fower men in different pairishes that whenever they hear o' my death, they'll cairry me up yonder and bury me there. And then I'll never leave it, but be still and quiet to the warld's end. I'll aye hae the sound o' water in my ear, for there's five burns tak' their rise on that hillside, and on a' airts the glens gang doun to the Gled and the Aller."

Then his spirit failed him, his voice sank, and he was almost the feeble gangrel once more. But not yet, for again his eye swept the ring of hills, and he muttered to himself names which I knew for streams, lingeringly, lovingly, as of old affections. "Aller and Gled and Callowa," he crooned, "braw names, and Clachlands and Cauldshaw and the Lanely Water. And I maunna forget the Stark and the Lin and the bonny streams o' the Creran. And what mair? I canna mind a' the burns, the Howe and the Hollies and the Fawn and the links o' the Manor. What says the Psalmist about them?

'As streams o' water in the South, Our bondage Lord, recall.'

Ay, but yen's the name for them. 'Streams o' water in the South.'"

And as we went down the slopes to the darkening vale I heard him crooning to himself in a high, quavering voice the single distich; then in a little his weariness took him again, and he plodded on with no thought save for his sorrows.

IV

The conclusion of this tale belongs not to me, but to the shepherd of the Redswirehead, and I heard it from him in his dwelling, as I stayed the night, belated on the darkening moors. He told me it after supper in a flood of misty Doric, and his voice grew rough at times, and he poked viciously at the dying peat.

In the last back-end I was at Gledfoot wi' sheep, and a weary job I had and little credit. Ye ken the place, a lang dreich shore wi' the wind swirlin' and bitin' to the bane, and the broun Gled water choked wi' Solloway sand. There was nae room in ony inn in the town, so I bude to gang to a bit public on the Harbour Walk, where sailor-folk and fishermen feucht and drank, and nae dacent men frae the hills thocht of gangin'. I was in a gey ill way, for I had sell't my beasts dooms cheap, and I thocht o' the lang miles hame in the wintry weather. So after a bite o' meat I gangs out to get the air and clear my heid, which was a' rammled wi' the auction-ring.

And whae did I find, sittin' on a bench at the door, but the auld man Yeddie. He was waur changed than ever. His lang hair was hingin' over his broo, and his face was thin and white as a ghaist's. His claes fell loose about him, and he sat wi' his hand on his auld stick and his chin on his hand, hearin' nocht and glowerin' afore him. He never saw nor kenned me till I shook him by the shoulders, and cried him by his name.

"Whae are ye?" says he, in a thin voice that gaed to my hert.

"Ye ken me fine, ye auld fule," says I. "I'm Jock Rorison o' the Redswirehead, whaur ye've stoppit often."

"Redswirehead," he says, like a man in a dream. "Redswirehead! That's at the tap o' the Clachlands Burn as ye gang ower to the Dreichil."

"And what are ye daein' here? It's no your countryside ava, and ye're no fit noo for lang trampin'."

"No," says he, in the same weak voice and wi' nae fushion in him, "but they winna hae me up yonder noo. I'm ower auld and useless. Yince a'body was gled to see me, and wad keep me as lang's I wantit, and had aye a gud word at meeting and pairting. Noo it's a' changed, and my wark's dune."

I saw fine that the man was daft, but what answer could I gie to his havers? Folk in the Callowa Glens are as kind as afore, but ill weather and auld age had put queer notions intil his heid. Forbye, he was seeck, seeck unto death, and I saw mair in his een than I likit to think.

"Come in-by and get some meat, man," I said. "Ye're famishin' wi' cauld and hunger."

"I canna eat," he says, and his voice never changed. "It's lang since I had a bite, for I'm no hungry. But I'm awfu' thirsty. I cam here yestreen, and I can get nae water to drink like the water in the hills. I maun be settin' out back the morn, if the Lord spares me."

I mindit fine that the body wad tak nae drink like an honest man, but maun aye draibble wi' burn water, and noo he had got the thing on the brain. I never spak a word, for the maitter was bye ony mortal's aid.

For lang he sat quiet. Then he lifts his heid and looks awa ower the grey sea. A licht for a moment cam intil his een.

"Whatna big water's yon?" he said, wi' his puir mind aye rinnin' on waters.

"That's the Solloway," says I.

"The Solloway," says he; " it's a big water, and it wad be an ill job to ford it."

"Nae man ever fordit it," I said.

"But I never yet cam to the water I couldna ford," says he. "But what's that queer smell i' the air? Something snell and cauld and unfreendly."

"That's the salt, for we're at the sea here, the mighty ocean.

He keepit repeatin' the word ower in his mouth. "The salt, the salt, I've heard tell o' it afore, but I dinna like it. It's terrible cauld and unhamely."

By this time an onding o' rain was coming up' frae the water, and I bade the man come indoors to the fire. He followed me, as biddable as a sheep, draggin' his legs like yin far gone in seeckness. I set him by the fire, and put whisky at his elbow, but he wadna touch it.

"I've nae need o' it," said he. "I'm find and warm"; and he sits staring at the fire, aye comin' ower again and again, "The Solloway, the Solloway. It's a guid name and a muckle water."

But sune I gaed to my bed, being heavy wi' sleep, for I had traivelled for twae days.

The next morn I was up at six and out to see the weather. It was a' changed. The muckle tides lay lang and still as our ain Loch o' the Lee, and far ayont I saw the big blue hills o' England shine bricht and clear. I thankit Providence for the day, for it was better to tak the lang miles back in sic a sun than in a blast o' rain.

But as I lookit I saw some folk comin' up frae the beach carryin' something atween them. My hert gied a loup, and " some puir, drooned sailor-body," says I to mysel', "whae has perished in yesterday's storm." But as they cam nearer I got a glisk which made me run like daft, and lang ere I was up on them I saw it was Yeddie.

He lay drippin' and white, wi' his puir auld hair lyin' back frae his broo and the duds clingin' to his legs. But out o' the face there had gane a' the seeckness and weariness. His een were stelled, as if he had been lookin' forrit to something, and his lips were set like a man on a lang errand. And mair, his stick was grippit sae firm in his hand that nae man could loose it, so they e'en let it be.

Then they tell't me the tale o't, how at the earliest licht they had seen him wanderin' alang the sands, juist as they were putting out their boats to sea. They wondered and watched him, till of a sudden he turned to the water and wadit in, keeping straucht on till he was oot o' sicht. They rowed a' their pith to the place, but they were ower late. Yince they saw his heid appear abune water, still wi' his face to the other side; and then they got his body, for the tide was rinnin' low in the mornin'. I tell't them a' I kenned o' him, and they were sair affected. "Puir cratur," said yin, "he's shurely better now."

So we brocht him up to the house and laid him there till the folk i' the town had heard o' the business. Syne the procurator-fiscal came and certifeed the death and the rest was left tae me. I got a wooden coffin made and put him in it, juist as he was, wi' his staff in his hand and his auld duds about him. I mindit o' my sworn word, for I was yin o' the four that had promised, and I ettled to dae his bidding. It was saxteen mile to the hills, and yin and twenty to the lanely tap whaur he had howkit his grave. But I never heedit it. I'm a strong man, weel-used to the walkin' and my hert was sair for the auld body. Now that he had gotten deliverance from his affliction, it was for me to leave him in the place he wantit. Forbye, he wasna muckle heavier than a bairn.

It was a long road, a sair road, but I did it, and by seven o'clock I was at the edge o' the muirlands. There was a braw mune, and a the glens and taps stood out as clear as midday. Bit by bit, for I was gey tired, I warstled ower the rigs and up the cleuchs to the Gled-head; syne up the stany Gled-cleuch to the lang grey hill which they ca' the Hurlybackit. By ten I had come to the cairn, and black i' the mune I saw the grave. So there I buried him, and though I'm no a releegious man, I couldna help sayin' ower him the guid words o' the Psalmist--

"As streams of water in the South, Our bondage, Lord, recall."

So if you go from the Gled to the Aller, and keep far over the north side of the Muckle Muneraw, you will come in time to a stony ridge which ends in a cairn. There you will see the whole hill country of the south, a hundred lochs, a myriad streams, and a forest of hill-tops. There on the very crest lies the old man, in the heart of his own land, at the fountain-head of his many waters. If you listen you will hear a hushed noise as of the swaying in trees or a ripple on the sea. It is the sound of the rising of burns, which, innumerable and unnumbered, flow thence to the silent glens for evermore.

THE GIPSY'S SONG TO THE LADY CASSILIS

"Whereupon the Faas, coming down fron the Gates of Galloway, did so bewitch my lady that she forgat husband and kin, and followed the tinkler's piping." --Chap-book of the Raid of Cassilis.

The door is open to the wall, The air is bright and free; Adown the stair, across the hall, And then-the world and me; The bare grey bent, the running stream, The fire beside the shore; And we will bid the hearth farewell, And never seek it more, My love, And never seek it more.

And you shall wear no silken gown, No maid shall bind your hair; The yellow broom shall be your gem, Your braid the heather rare. Athwart the moor, adown the hill, Across the world away; The path is long for happy hearts That sing to greet the day, My love, That sing to greet the day.

When morning cleaves the eastern grey, And the lone hills are red When sunsets light the evening way And birds are quieted; In autumn noon and springtide dawn, By hill and dale and sea, The world shall sing its ancient song Of hope and joy for thee, My love, Of hope and joy for thee.

And at the last no solemn stole Shall on thy breast be laid; No mumbling priest shall speed thy soul, No charnel vault thee shade. But by the shadowed hazel copse, Aneath the greenwood tree, Where airs are soft and waters sing, Thou'lt ever sleep by me, My love, Thou'lt ever sleep by me.

THE GROVE OF ASHTAROTH
VI

"C'est enfin que dans leurs prunelles Rit et pleure-fastidieux-- L'amour des choses eternelles Des vieux morts et des anciens dieux!"
--PAUL VERLAINE.

We were sitting around the camp fire, some thirty miles north of a place called Taqui, when Lawson announced his intention of finding a home. He had spoken little the last day or two, and I had guessed that he had struck a vein of private reflection. I thought it might be a new mine or irrigation scheme, and I was surprised to find that it was a country house.

"I don't think I shall go back to England," he said, kicking a sputtering log into place. "I don't see why I should. For business purposes I am far more useful to the firm in South Africa than in Throgmorton Street. I have no relation left except a third cousin, and I have never cared a rush for living in town. That beastly house of mine in Hill Street will fetch what I gave for it,--Isaacson cabled about it the other day, offering for furniture and all. I don't want to go into Parliament, and I hate shooting little birds and tame deer. I am one of those fellows who are born Colonial at heart, and I don't see why I shouldn't arrange my life as I please. Besides, for ten years I have been falling in love with this country, and now I am up to the neck."

He flung himself back in the camp-chair till the canvas creaked, and looked at me below his eyelids. I remember glancing at the lines of him, and thinking what a fine make of a man he was. In his untanned field-boots, breeches, and grey shirt, he looked the born wilderness hunter, though less than two months before he had been driving down to the City every morning in the sombre regimentals of his class. Being a fair man, he was gloriously tanned, and there was a clear line at his shirt-collar to mark the limits of his sunburn. I had first known him years ago, when he was a broker's clerk working on half-commission. Then he had gone to South Africa, and soon I heard he was a partner in a mining house which was doing wonders with some gold areas in the North. The next step was his return to London as the new millionaire,--young, good-looking, wholesome in mind and body, and much sought after by the mothers of marriageable girls. We played polo together, and hunted a little in the season, but there were signs that he did not propose to become the conventional English gentleman. He refused to buy a place in the country, though half the Homes of England were at his disposal. He was a very busy man, he declared, and had not time to be a squire. Besides, every few months he used to rush out to South Africa. I saw that he was restless, for he was always badgering me to go big-game hunting with him in some remote part of the earth. There was that in his eyes, too, which marked him out from the ordinary blond type of our countrymen. They were large and brown and mysterious, and the light of another race was in their odd depths.

To hint such a thing would have meant a breach of friendship, for Lawson was very proud of his birth. When he first made his fortune he had gone to the Heralds to discover his family, and these obliging gentlemen had provided a pedigree. It appeared that he was a scion of the house of Lowson or Lowieson, an ancient and rather disreputable clan on the Scottish side of the Border. He took a shooting in Teviotdale on the strength of it, and used to commit lengthy Border ballads to memory. But I had known his father, a financial journalist who never quite succeeded, and I had heard of a grandfather who sold antiques in a back street at Brighton. The latter, I think, had not changed his name, and still frequented the synagogue. The father was a progressive Christian, and the mother had been a blonde Saxon from the Midlands. In my mind there was no doubt, as I caught Lawson's heavy-lidded eyes fixed on me. My friend was of a more ancient race than the Lowsons of the Border.

"Where are you thinking of looking for your house?" I asked. "In Natal or in the Cape Peninsula? You might get the Fishers' place if you paid a price."

"The Fishers' place be hanged!" he said crossly. "I don't want any stuccoed, over-grown Dutch farm. I might as well be at Roehampton as in the Cape."

He got up and walked to the far side of the fire, where a lane ran down through the thornscrub to a gully of the hills. The moon was silvering the bush of the plains, forty miles off and three thousand feet below us.

"I am going to live somewhere hereabouts," he answered at last. I whistled. "Then you've got to put your hand in your pocket, old man. You'll have to make everything, including a map of the countryside."

"I know," he said; "that's where the fun comes in. Hang it all, why shouldn't I indulge my fancy? I'm uncommonly well off, and I haven't chick or child to leave it to. Supposing I'm a hundred miles from rail-head, what about it? I'll make a motor-road and fix up a telephone. I'll grow most of my supplies, and start a colony to provide labour. When you come and stay with me, you'll get the best food and drink on earth, and sport that will make your mouth water. I'll put Lochleven trout in these streams,--at 6,000 feet you can do anything. We'll have a pack of hounds, too, and we can drive pig in the woods, and if we want big game there are the Mangwe flats at our feet. I tell you I'll make such a country-house as nobody ever dreamed of. A man will come plumb out of stark savagery into lawns and rose-gardens." Lawson flung himself into his chair again and smiled dreamily at the fire.

"But why here, of all places?" I persisted. I was not feeling very well and did not care for the country.

"I can't quite explain. I think it's the sort of land I have always been looking for. I always fancied a house on a green plateau in a decent climate looking down on the tropics. I like heat and colour, you know, but I like hills too, and greenery, and the things that bring back Scotland. Give me a cross between Teviotdale and the Orinoco, and, by Gad! I think I've got it here."

I watched my friend curiously, as with bright eyes and eager voice he talked of his new fad. The two races were very clear in him--the one desiring gorgeousness, the other athirst for the soothing spaces of the North. He began to plan out the house. He would get Adamson to design it, and it was to grow out of the landscape like a stone on the hillside. There would be wide verandahs and cool halls, but great fireplaces against winter time. It would all be very simple and fresh--"clean as morning" was his odd phrase; but then another idea supervened, and he talked of bringing the Tintorets from Hill Street. "I want it to be a civilised house, you know. No silly luxury, but the best pictures and china and books. I'll have all the furniture made after the old plain English models out of native woods. I don't want second-hand sticks in a new country. Yes, by Jove, the Tintorets are a great idea, and all those Ming pots I bought. I had meant to sell them, but I'll have them out here."

He talked for a good hour of what he would do, and his dream grew richer as he talked, till by the time we went to bed he had sketched something more like a palace than a country-house. Lawson was by no means a luxurious man. At present he was well content with a Wolseley valise, and shaved cheerfully out of a tin mug. It struck me as odd that a man so simple in his habits should have so sumptuous a taste in bric-a-brac. I told myself, as I turned in, that the Saxon mother from the Midlands had done little to dilute the strong wine of the East.

It drizzled next morning when we inspanned, and I mounted my horse in a bad temper. I had some fever on me, I think, and I hated this lush yet frigid tableland, where all the winds on earth lay in wait for one's marrow. Lawson was, as usual, in great spirits. We were not hunting, but shifting our hunting-ground, so all morning we travelled fast to the north along the rim of the uplands.

At midday it cleared, and the afternoon was a pageant of pure colour. The wind sank to a low breeze; the sun lit the infinite green spaces, and kindled the wet forest to a jewelled coronal. Lawson gaspingly admired it all, as he cantered bareheaded up a bracken-clad slope. "God's country," he said twenty times. "I've found it." Take a piece of Sussex downland; put a stream in every hollow and a patch of wood; and at the edge, where the cliffs at home would fall to the sea, put a cloak of forest muffling the scarp and dropping thousands of feet to the blue plains. Take the diamond air of the Gornergrat, and the riot of colour which you get by a West Highland lochside in late September. Put flowers everywhere, the things we grow in hothouses, geraniums like sun-shades and arums like trumpets. That will give you a notion of the countryside we were in. I began to see that after all it was out of the common.

And just before sunset we came over a ridge and found something better. It was a shallow glen, half a mile wide, down which ran a blue-grey stream in lings like the Spean, till at the edge of the plateau it leaped into the dim forest in a snowy cascade. The opposite side ran up in gentle slopes to a rocky knell, from which the eye had a noble prospect of the plains. All down the glen were little copses, half moons of green edging some silvery shore of the burn, or delicate clusters of tall trees nodding on the hill brow. The place so satisfied the eye that for the sheer wonder of its perfection we stopped and stared in silence for many minutes.

Then "The House," I said, and Lawson replied softly, "The House!"

We rode slowly into the glen in the mulberry gloaming. Our transport waggons were half an hour behind, so we had time to explore. Lawson dismounted and plucked handfuls of flowers from the water meadows. He was singing to himself all the time--an old French catch about Cadet Rousselle and his Trois maisons.

"Who owns it?" I asked.

"My firm, as like as not. We have miles of land about here. But whoever the man is, he has got to sell. Here I build my tabernacle, old man. Here, and nowhere else!"

In the very centre of the glen, in a loop of the stream, was one copse which even in that half light struck me as different from the others. It was of tall, slim, fairy-like trees, the kind of wood the monks painted in old missals. No, I rejected the thought. It was no Christian wood. It was not a copse, but a "grove,"--one such as Artemis may have flitted through in the moonlight. It was small, forty or fifty yards in diameter, and there was a dark something at the heart of it which for a second I thought was a house.

We turned between the slender trees, and--was it fancy?--an odd tremor went through me. I felt as if I were penetrating the temenos of some strange and lovely divinity, the goddess of this pleasant vale. There was a spell in the air, it seemed, and an odd dead silence.

Suddenly my horse started at a flutter of light wings. A flock of doves rose from the branches, and I saw the burnished green of their plumes against the opal sky. Lawson did not seem to notice them. I saw his keen eyes staring at the centre of the grove and what stood there.

It was a little conical tower, ancient and lichened, but, so far as I could judge, quite flawless. You know the famous Conical Temple at Zimbabwe, of which prints are in every guidebook. This was of the same type, but a thousandfold more perfect. It stood about thirty feet high, of solid masonry, without door or window or cranny, as shapely as when it first came from the hands of the old builders. Again I had the sense of breaking in on a sanctuary. What right had I, a common vulgar modern, to be looking at this fair thing, among these delicate trees, which some white goddess had once taken for her shrine?

Lawson broke in on my absorption. "Let's get out of this," he said hoarsely and he took my horse's bridle (he had left his own beast at the edge) and led him back to the open. But I noticed that his eyes were always turning back and that his hand trembled.

"That settles it," I said after supper. "What do you want with your mediaeval Venetians and your Chinese pots now? You will have the finest antique in the world in your garden--a temple as old as time, and in a land which they say has no history. You had the right inspiration this time."

I think I have said that Lawson had hungry eyes. In his enthusiasm they used to glow and brighten; but now, as he sat looking down at the olive shades of the glen, they seemed ravenous in their fire. He had hardly spoken a word since we left the wood.

"Where can I read about these things?" he asked, and I gave him the names of books. Then, an hour later, he asked me who were the builders. I told him the little I knew about Phoenician and Sabaen wanderings, and the ritual of Sidon and Tyre. He repeated some names to himself and went soon to bed.

As I turned in, I had one last look over the glen, which lay ivory and black in the moon. I seemed to hear a faint echo of wings, and to see over the little grove a cloud of light visitants. "The Doves of Ashtaroth have come back," I said to myself. "It is a good omen. They accept the new tenant." But as I fell asleep I had a sudden thought that I was saying something rather terrible.

II

Three years later, pretty nearly to a day, I came back to see what Lawson had made of his hobby. He had bidden me often to Welgevonden, as he chose to call it--though I do not know why he should have fixed a

THE MOON ENDURETH

Dutch name to a countryside where Boer never trod. At the last there had been some confusion about dates, and I wired the time of my arrival, and set off without an answer. A motor met me at the queer little wayside station of Taqui, and after many miles on a doubtful highway I came to the gates of the park, and a road on which it was a delight to move. Three years had wrought little difference in the landscape. Lawson had done some planting,--conifers and flowering shrubs and suchlike,--but wisely he had resolved that Nature had for the most part forestalled him. All the same, he must have spent a mint of money. The drive could not have been beaten in England, and fringes of mown turf on either hand had been pared out of the lush meadows. When we came over the edge of the hill and looked down on the secret glen, I could not repress a cry of pleasure. The house stood on the farther ridge, the viewpoint of the whole neighbourhood; and its brown timbers and white rough-cast walls melted into the hillside as if it had been there from the beginning of things. The vale below was ordered in lawns and gardens. A blue lake received the rapids of the stream, and its banks were a maze of green shades and glorious masses of blossom. I noticed, too, that the little grove we had explored on our first visit stood alone in a big stretch of lawn, so that its perfection might be clearly seen. Lawson had excellent taste, or he had had the best advice.

The butler told me that his master was expected home shortly, and took me into the library for tea. Lawson had left his Tintorets and Ming pots at home after all. It was a long, low room, panelled in teak half-way up the walls, and the shelves held a multitude of fine bindings. There were good rugs on the parquet door, but no ornaments anywhere, save three. On the carved mantelpiece stood two of the old soapstone birds which they used to find at Zimbabwe, and between, on an ebony stand, a half moon of alabaster, curiously carved with zodiacal figures. My host had altered his scheme of furnishing, but I approved the change.

He came in about half-past six, after I had consumed two cigars and all but fallen asleep. Three years make a difference in most men, but I was not prepared for the change in Lawson. For one thing, he had grown fat. In place of the lean young man I had known, I saw a heavy, flaccid being, who shuffled in his gait, and seemed tired and listless. His sunburn had gone, and his face was as pasty as a city clerk's. He had been walking, and wore shapeless flannel clothes, which hung loose even on his enlarged figure. And the worst of it was, that he did not seem overpleased to see me. He murmured something about my journey, and then flung himself into an arm-chair and looked out of the window.

I asked him if he had been ill.

"Ill! No!" he said crossly. "Nothing of the kind. I'm perfectly well."

"You don't look as fit as this place should make you. What do you do with yourself? Is the shooting as good as you hoped?"

He did not answer, but I thought I heard him mutter something like "shooting be damned."

Then I tried the subject of the house. I praised it extravagantly, but with conviction. "There can be no place like it in the world," I said.

He turned his eyes on me at last, and I saw that they were as deep and restless as ever. With his pallid face they made him look curiously Semitic. I had been right in my theory about his ancestry.

"Yes," he said slowly, "there is no place like it--in the world."

Then he pulled himself to his feet. "I'm going to change," he said. "Dinner is at eight. Ring for Travers, and he'll show you your room."

I dressed in a noble bedroom, with an outlook over the garden-vale and the escarpment to the far line of the plains, now blue and saffron in the sunset. I dressed in an ill temper, for I was seriously offended with Lawson, and also seriously alarmed. He was either very unwell or going out of his mind, and it was clear, too, that he would resent any anxiety on his account. I ransacked my memory for rumours, but found none. I had heard nothing of him except that he had been extraordinarily successful in his speculations, and that from his hill-top he directed his firm's operations with uncommon skill. If Lawson was sick or mad, nobody knew of it.

Dinner was a trying ceremony. Lawson, who used to be rather particular in his dress, appeared in a kind of smoking suit with a flannel collar. He spoke scarcely a word to me, but cursed the servants with a brutality which left me aghast. A wretched footman in his nervousness spilt some sauce over his sleeve. Lawson dashed the dish from his hand and volleyed abuse with a sort of epileptic fury. Also he, who had been the most abstemious of men, swallowed disgusting quantities of champagne and old brandy.

He had given up smoking, and half an hour after we left the dining-room he announced his intention of going to bed. I watched him as he waddled upstairs with a feeling of angry bewilderment. Then I went to the library and lit a pipe. I would leave first thing in the morning--on that I was determined. But as I sat gazing at the moon of alabaster and the soapstone birds my anger evaporated, and concern took its place. I remembered what a fine fellow Lawson had been, what good times we had had together. I remembered especially that evening when we had found this valley and given rein to our fancies. What horrid alchemy in the place had turned a gentleman into a brute? I thought of drink and drugs and madness and insomnia, but I could fit none of them into my conception of my friend. I did not consciously rescind my resolve to depart, but I had a notion that I would not act on it.

The sleepy butler met me as I went to bed. "Mr. Lawson's room is at the end of your corridor, sir," he said. "He don't sleep over well, so you may hear him stirring in the night. At what hour would you like breakfast, sir? Mr. Lawson mostly has his in bed."

My room opened from the great corridor, which ran the full length of the front of the house. So far as I could make out, Lawson was three rooms off, a vacant bedroom and his servant's room being between us. I felt tired and cross, and tumbled into bed as fast as possible. Usually I sleep well, but now I was soon conscious that my drowsiness was wearing off and that I was in for a restless night. I got up and laved my face, turned the pillows, thought of sheep coming over a hill and clouds crossing the sky; but none of the old devices were of any use. After about an hour of make-believe I surrendered myself to facts, and, lying on my back, stared at the white ceiling and the patches of moonshine on the walls.

It certainly was an amazing night. I got up, put on a dressing-gown, and drew a chair to the window. The moon was almost at its full, and the whole plateau swam in a radiance of ivory and silver. The banks of the stream were black, but the lake had a great belt of light athwart it, which made it seem like a horizon and the rim of land beyond it like a contorted cloud. Far to the right I saw the delicate outlines of the little wood which I had come to think of as the Grove of Ashtaroth. I listened. There was not a sound in the air. The land seemed to sleep peacefully beneath the moon, and yet I had a sense that the peace was an illusion. The place was feverishly restless.

I could have given no reason for my impression but there it was. Something was stirring in the wide moonlit landscape under its deep mask of silence. I felt as I had felt on the evening three years ago when I had ridden into the grove. I did not think that the influence, whatever it was, was maleficent. I only knew that it was very strange, and kept me wakeful.

By-and-by I bethought me of a book. There was no lamp in the corridor save the moon, but the whole house was bright as I slipped down the great staircase and across the hall to the library. I switched on the lights and then switched them off. They seemed profanation, and I did not need them.

I found a French novel, but the place held me and I stayed. I sat down in an arm-chair before the fireplace and the stone birds. Very odd those gawky things, like prehistoric Great Auks, looked in the moonlight. I remember that the alabaster moon shimmered like translucent pearl, and I fell to wondering about its history. Had the old Sabaens used such a jewel in their rites in the Grove of Ashtaroth?

Then I heard footsteps pass the window. A great house like this would have a watchman, but these quick shuffling footsteps were surely not the dull plod of a servant. They passed on to the grass and died away. I began to think of getting back to my room.

In the corridor I noticed that Lawson's door was ajar, and that a light had been left burning. I had the unpardonable curiosity to peep in. The room was empty, and the bed had not been slept in. Now I knew whose were the footsteps outside the library window.

I lit a reading-lamp and tried to interest myself in "La Cruelle Enigme." But my wits were restless, and I could not keep my eyes on the page. I flung the book aside and sat down again by the window. The feeling came over me that I was sitting in a box at some play. The glen was a huge stage, and at any moment the players might appear on it. My attention was strung as high as if I had been waiting for the advent of some world-famous actress. But nothing came. Only the shadows shifted and lengthened as the moon moved across the sky.

Then quite suddenly the restlessness left me and at the same moment the silence was broken by the crow of a cock and the rustling of trees in a light wind. I felt very sleepy, and was turning to bed when again I heard footsteps without. From the window I could see a figure moving across the garden towards the house. It was Lawson, got up in the sort of towel dressing-gown that one wears on board ship. He was walking slowly and painfully, as if very weary. I did not see his face, but the man's whole air was that of extreme fatigue and dejection. I tumbled into bed and slept profoundly till long after daylight.

III

The man who valeted me was Lawson's own servant. As he was laying out my clothes I asked after the health of his master, and was told that he had slept ill and would not rise till late. Then the man, an anxious-faced Englishman, gave me some information on his own account. Mr. Lawson was having one of his bad turns. It would pass away in a day or two, but till it had gone he was fit for nothing. He advised me to see Mr. Jobson, the factor, who would look to my entertainment in his master's absence.

Jobson arrived before luncheon, and the sight of him was the first satisfactory thing about Welgevonden. He was a big, gruff Scot from Roxburghshire, engaged, no doubt, by Lawson as a duty to his Border ancestry. He had short grizzled whiskers, a weatherworn face, and a shrewd, calm blue eye. I knew now why the place was in such perfect order.

We began with sport, and Jobson explained what I could have in the way of fishing and shooting. His exposition was brief and business-like, and all the while I could see his eye searching me. It was clear that he had much to say on other matters than sport.

I told him that I had come here with Lawson three years before, when he chose the site. Jobson continued to regard me curiously. "I've heard tell of ye from Mr. Lawson. Ye're an old friend of his, I understand."

"The oldest," I said. "And I am sorry to find that the place does not agree with him. Why it doesn't I cannot imagine, for you look fit enough. Has he been seedy for long?"

"It comes and it goes," said Mr. Jobson. "Maybe once a month he has a bad turn. But on the whole it agrees with him badly. He's no' the man he was when I first came here."

Jobson was looking at me very seriously and frankly. I risked a question.

"What do you suppose is the matter?"

He did not reply at once, but leaned forward and tapped my knee. "I think it's something that doctors canna cure. Look at me, sir. I've always been counted a sensible man, but if I told you what was in my head you would think me daft. But I have one word for you. Bide till to-night is past and then speir your question. Maybe you and me will be agreed."

The factor rose to go. As he left the room he flung me back a remark over his shoulder--"Read the eleventh chapter of the First Book of Kings."

After luncheon I went for a walk. First I mounted to the crown of the hill and feasted my eyes on the unequalled loveliness of the view. I saw the far hills in Portuguese territory, a hundred miles away, lifting up thin blue fingers into the sky. The wind blew light and fresh, and the place was fragrant with a thousand delicate scents. Then I descended to the vale, and followed the stream up through the garden. Poinsettias and oleanders were blazing in coverts, and there was a paradise of tinted water-lilies in the slacker reaches. I saw good trout rise at the fly, but I did not think about fishing. I was searching my memory for a recollection which would not come. By-and-by I found myself beyond the garden, where the lawns ran to the fringe of Ashtaroth's Grove.

It was like something I remembered in an old Italian picture. Only, as my memory drew it, it should have been peopled with strange figures-nymphs dancing on the sward, and a prick-eared faun peeping from the covert. In the warm afternoon sunlight it stood, ineffably gracious and beautiful, tantalising with a sense of some deep hidden loveliness. Very reverently I walked between the slim trees, to where the little conical tower stood half in the sun and half in shadow. Then I noticed something new. Round the tower ran a narrow path, worn in the grass by human feet. There had been no such path on my first visit, for I remembered the grass growing tall to the edge of the stone. Had the Kaffirs made a shrine of it, or were there other and strange votaries?

When I returned to the house I found Travers with a message for me. Mr. Lawson was still in bed, but he would like me to go to him. I found my friend sitting up and drinking strong tea,--a bad thing, I should have thought, for a man in his condition. I remember that I looked about the room for some sign of the pernicious habit of which I believed him a victim. But the place was fresh and clean, with the windows wide open, and, though I could not have given my reasons, I was convinced that drugs or drink had nothing to do with the sickness.

He received me more civilly, but I was shocked by his looks. There were great bags below his eyes, and his skin had the wrinkled puffy appearance of a man in dropsy. His voice, too, was reedy and thin. Only his great eyes burned with some feverish life.

"I am a shocking bad host," he said, "but I'm going to be still more inhospitable. I want you to go away. I hate anybody here when I'm off colour."

"Nonsense," I said; "you want looking after. I want to know about this sickness. Have you had a doctor?"

He smiled wearily. "Doctors are no earthly use to me. There's nothing much the matter I tell you. I'll be all right in a day or two, and then you can come back. I want you to go off with Jobson and hunt in the plains till the end of the week. It will be better fun for you, and I'll feel less guilty."

Of course I pooh-poohed the idea, and Lawson got angry. "Damn it, man," he cried, "why do you force yourself on me when I don't want you? I tell you your presence here makes me worse. In a week I'll be as right as the mail and then I'll be thankful for you. But get away now; get away, I tell you."

I saw that he was fretting himself into a passion. "All right," I said soothingly; "Jobson and I will go off hunting. But I am horribly anxious about you, old man."

He lay back on his pillows. "You needn't trouble. I only want a little rest. Jobson will make all arrangements, and Travers will get you anything you want. Good-bye."

I saw it was useless to stay longer, so I left the room. Outside I found the anxious-faced servant "Look here," I said, "Mr. Lawson thinks I ought to go, but I mean to stay. Tell him I'm gone if he asks you. And for Heaven's sake keep him in bed."

The man promised, and I thought I saw some relief in his face.

I went to the library, and on the way remembered Jobson's remark about Ist Kings. With some searching I found a Bible and turned up the passage. It was a long screed about the misdeeds of Solomon, and I read it through without enlightenment. I began to re-read it, and a word suddenly caught my attention--

"For Solomon went after Ashtaroth, the goddess of the Zidonians."

That was all, but it was like a key to a cipher. Instantly there flashed over my mind all that I had heard or read of that strange ritual which seduced Israel to sin. I saw a sunburnt land and a people vowed to the stern service of Jehovah. But I saw, too, eyes turning from the austere sacrifice to lonely hill-top groves and towers and images, where dwelt some subtle and evil mystery. I saw the fierce prophets, scourging the votaries with rods, and a nation Penitent before the Lord; but always the backsliding again, and the hankering after forbidden joys. Ashtaroth was the old goddess of the East. Was it not possible that in all Semitic blood there remained transmitted through the dim generations, some craving for her spell? I thought of the grandfather in the back street at Brighten and of those burning eyes upstairs.

As I sat and mused my glance fell on the inscrutable stone birds. They knew all those old secrets of joy and terror. And that moon of alabaster! Some dark priest had worn it on his forehead when he worshipped, like Ahab, "all the host of Heaven." And then I honestly began to be afraid. I, a prosaic, modern Christian gentleman, a half-believer in casual faiths,

THE MOON ENDURETH

was in the presence of some hoary mystery of sin far older than creeds or Christendom. There was fear in my heart--a kind of uneasy disgust, and above all a nervous eerie disquiet. Now I wanted to go away and yet I was ashamed of the cowardly thought. I pictured Ashtaroth's Grove with sheer horror. What tragedy was in the air? What secret awaited twilight? For the night was coming, the night of the Full Moon, the season of ecstasy and sacrifice.

I do not know how I got through that evening. I was disinclined for dinner, so I had a cutlet in the library and sat smoking till my tongue ached. But as the hours passed a more manly resolution grew up in my mind. I owed it to old friendship to stand by Lawson in this extremity. I could not interfere--God knows, his reason seemed already rocking, but I could be at hand in case my chance came. I determined not to undress, but to watch through the night. I had a bath, and changed into light flannels and slippers. Then I took up my position in a corner of the library close to the window, so that I could not fail to hear Lawson's footsteps if he passed.

Fortunately I left the lights unlit, for as I waited I grew drowsy, and fell asleep. When I woke the moon had risen, and I knew from the feel of the air that the hour was late. I sat very still, straining my ears, and as I listened I caught the sound of steps. They were crossing the hall stealthily, and nearing the library door. I huddled into my corner as Lawson entered.

He wore the same towel dressing-gown, and he moved swiftly and silently as if in a trance. I watched him take the alabaster moon from the mantelpiece and drop it in his pocket. A glimpse of white skin showed that the gown was his only clothing. Then he moved past me to the window, opened it and went out.

Without any conscious purpose I rose and followed, kicking off my slippers that I might go quietly. He was running, running fast, across the lawns in the direction of the Grove--an odd shapeless antic in the moonlight. I stopped, for there was no cover, and I feared for his reason if he saw me. When I looked again he had disappeared among the trees.

I saw nothing for it but to crawl, so on my belly I wormed my way over the dripping sward. There was a ridiculous suggestion of deer-stalking about the game which tickled me and dispelled my uneasiness. Almost I persuaded myself I was tracking an ordinary sleep-walker. The lawns were broader than I imagined, and it seemed an age before I reached the edge of the Grove. The world was so still that I appeared to be making a most ghastly amount of noise. I remember that once I heard a rustling in the air, and looked up to see the green doves circling about the tree-tops.

There was no sign of Lawson. On the edge of the Grove I think that all my assurance vanished. I could see between the trunks to the little tower, but it was quiet as the grave, save for the wings above. Once more there came over me the unbearable sense of anticipation I had felt the night before. My nerves tingled with mingled expectation and dread. I did not think that any harm would come to me, for the powers of the air seemed not malignant. But I knew them for powers, and felt awed and abased. I was in the presence of the "host of Heaven," and I was no stern Israelitish prophet to prevail against them.

I must have lain for hours waiting in that spectral place, my eyes riveted on the tower and its golden cap of moonshine. I remember that my head felt void and light, as if my spirit were becoming disembodied and leaving its dew-drenched sheath far below. But the most curious sensation was of something drawing me to the tower, something mild and kindly and rather feeble, for there was some other and stronger force keeping me back. I yearned to move nearer, but I could not drag my limbs an inch. There was a spell somewhere which I could not break. I do not think I was in any way frightened now. The starry influence was playing tricks with me, but my mind was half asleep. Only I never took my eyes from the little tower. I think I could not, if I had wanted to.

Then suddenly from the shadows came Lawson. He was stark-naked, and he wore, bound across his brow, the half-moon of alabaster. He had something, too, in his hand,--something which glittered.

He ran round the tower, crooning to himself, and flinging wild arms to the skies. Sometimes the crooning changed to a shrill cry of passion, such as a manad may have uttered in the train of Bacchus. I could make out no words, but the sound told its own tale. He was absorbed in some infernal ecstasy. And as he ran, he drew his right hand across his breast and arms, and I saw that it held a knife.

I grew sick with disgust,--not terror, but honest physical loathing. Lawson, gashing his fat body, affected me with an overpowering repugnance. I wanted to go forward and stop him, and I wanted, too, to be a hundred miles away. And the result was that I stayed still. I believe my own will held me there, but I doubt if in any case I could have moved my legs.

The dance grew swifter and fiercer. I saw the blood dripping from Lawson's body, and his face ghastly white above his scarred breast. And then suddenly the horror left me; my head swam; and for one second--one brief second--I seemed to peer into a new world. A strange passion surged up in my heart. I seemed to see the earth peopled with forms not human, scarcely divine, but more desirable than man or god. The calm face of Nature broke up for me into wrinkles of wild knowledge. I saw the things which brush against the soul in dreams, and found them lovely. There seemed no cruelty in the knife or the blood. It was a delicate mystery of worship, as wholesome as the morning song of birds. I do not know how the Semites found Ashtaroth's ritual; to them it may well have been more rapt and passionate than it seemed to me. For I saw in it only the sweet simplicity of Nature, and all riddles of lust and terror soothed away as a child's nightmares are calmed by a mother. I found my legs able to move, and I think I took two steps through the dusk towards the tower.

And then it all ended. A cock crew, and the homely noises of earth were renewed. While I stood dazed and shivering, Lawson plunged through the Grove toward me. The impetus carried him to the edge, and he fell fainting just outside the shade.

My wits and common-sense came back to me with my bodily strength. I got my friend on my back, and staggered with him towards the house. I was afraid in real earnest now, and what frightened me most was the thought that I had not been afraid sooner. I had come very near the "abomination of the Zidonians."

At the door I found the scared valet waiting. He had apparently done this sort of thing before

"Your master has been sleep-walking and has had a fall," I said. "We must get him to bed at once."

We bathed the wounds as he lay in a deep stupor, and I dressed them as well as I could. The only danger lay in his utter exhaustion, for happily the gashes were not serious, and no artery had been touched. Sleep and rest would make him well, for he had the constitution of a strong man. I was leaving the room when he opened his eyes and spoke. He did not recognize me, but I noticed that his face had lost its strangeness, and was once more that of the friend I had known. Then I suddenly bethought me of an old hunting remedy which he and I always carried on our expeditions. It is a pill made up from an ancient Portuguese prescription. One is an excellent specific for fever. Two are invaluable if you are lost in the bush, for they send a man for many hours into a deep sleep, which prevents suffering and madness, till help comes. Three give a painless death. I went to my room and found the little box in my jewel-case. Lawson swallowed two, and turned wearily on his side. I bade his man let him sleep till he woke, and went off in search of food.

IV

I had business on hand which would not wait. By seven, Jobson, who had been sent for, was waiting for me in the library. I knew by his grim face that here I had a very good substitute for a prophet of the Lord.

"You were right," I said. "I have read the IIth chapter of Ist Kings, and I have spent such a night as I pray God I shall never spend again.

"I thought you would," he replied. "I've had the same experience myself."

"The Grove?" I said.

"Ay, the wud," was the answer in broad Scots.

I wanted to see how much he understood. "Mr. Lawson's family is from the Scottish Border?"

"Ay. I understand they come off Borthwick Water side," he replied, but I saw by his eyes that he knew what I meant.

"Mr. Lawson is my oldest friend," I went on, "and I am going to take measures to cure him. For what I am going to do I take the sole responsibility. I will make that plain to your master. But if I am to succeed I want your help. Will you give it me? It sounds like madness and you are a sensible man and may like to keep out of it. I leave it to your discretion."

Jobson looked me straight in the face. "Have no fear for me," he said; "there is an unholy thing in that place, and if I have the strength in me I will destroy it. He has been a good master to me, and, forbye I am a believing Christian. So say on, sir."

There was no mistaking the air. I had found my Tishbite.

"I want men," I said, "--as many as we can get."

Jobson mused. "The Kaffirs will no' gang near the place, but there's some thirty white men on the tobacco farm. They'll do your will, if you give them an indemnity in writing."

"Good," said I. "Then we will take our instructions from the only authority which meets the case. We will follow the example of King Josiah. I turned up the 23rd chapter of end Kings, and read--

"And the high places that were before Jerusalem, which were on the right hand of the Mount of Corruption, which Solomon the king of Israel had built for Ashtaroth the abomination of the Zidonians ... did the king defile.

"And he brake in Pieces the images, and cut down the groves. and filled their places with the bones of men....'

"Moreover the altar that was at Beth-el, and the high place which Jeroboam the son of Nebat, who made Israel to sin, had made, both that altar and the high place he brake down, and burned the high place, and stamped it small to powder, and burned the grove."

Jobson nodded. "It'll need dinnymite. But I've plenty of yon down at the workshops. I'll be off to collect the lads."

Before nine the men had assembled at Jobson's house. They were a hardy lot of young farmers from home, who took their instructions docilely from the masterful factor. On my orders they had brought their shotguns. We armed them with spades and woodmen's axes, and one man wheeled some coils of rope in a handcart.

In the clear, windless air of morning the Grove, set amid its lawns, looked too innocent and exquisite for ill. I had a pang of regret that a thing so fair should suffer; nay, if I had come alone, I think I might have repented. But the men were there, and the grim-faced Jobson was waiting for orders. I placed the guns, and sent beaters to the far side. I told them that every dove must be shot.

It was only a small flock, and we killed fifteen at the first drive. The poor birds flew over the glen to another spinney, but we brought them back over the guns and seven fell. Four more were got in the trees, and the last I killed myself with a long shot. In half an hour there was a pile of little green bodies on the sward.

Then we went to work to cut down the trees. The slim stems were an easy task to a good woodman, and one after another they toppled to the ground. And meantime, as I watched, I became conscious of a strange emotion.

It was as if someone were pleading with me. A gentle voice, not threatening, but pleading--something too fine for the sensual ear, but touching inner chords of the spirit. So tenuous it was and distant that I could think of no personality behind it. Rather it was the viewless, bodiless grace of this delectable vale, some old exquisite divinity of the groves. There was the heart of all sorrow in it, and the soul of all loveliness. It seemed a woman's voice, some lost lady who had brought nothing but goodness unrepaid to the world. And what the voice told me was that I was destroying her last shelter.

That was the pathos of it--the voice was homeless. As the axes flashed in the sunlight and the wood grew thin, that gentle spirit was pleading with me for mercy and a brief respite. It seemed to be telling of a world for centuries grown coarse and pitiless, of long sad wanderings, of hardly-won shelter, and a peace which was the little all she sought from men. There was nothing terrible in it. No thought of wrong-doing. The spell, which to Semitic blood held the mystery of evil, was to me, of the Northern race, only delicate and rare and beautiful. Jobson and the rest did not feel it, I with my finer senses caught nothing but the hopeless sadness of it. That which had stirred the passion in Lawson was only wringing my heart. It was almost too pitiful to bear. As the trees crashed down and the men wiped the sweat from their brows, I seemed to myself like the murderer of fair women and innocent children. I remember that the tears were running over my cheeks. More than once I opened my mouth to countermand the work, but the face of Jobson, that grim Tishbite, held me back.

I knew now what gave the Prophets of the Lord their mastery, and I knew also why the people sometimes stoned them.

The last tree fell, and the little tower stood like a ravished shrine, stripped of all defence against the world. I heard Jobson's voice speaking. "We'd better blast that stane thing now. We'll trench on four sides and lay the dinnymite. Ye're no' looking weel, sir.!Ye'd better go and sit down on the braeface."

I went up the hillside and lay down. Below me, in the waste of shorn trunks, men were running about, and I saw the mining begin. It all seemed like an aimless dream in which I had no part. The voice of that homeless goddess was still pleading. It was the innocence of it that tortured me Even so must a merciful Inquisitor have suffered from the plea of some fair girl with the aureole of death on her hair. I knew I was killing rare and unrecoverable beauty. As I sat dazed and heartsick, the whole loveliness of Nature seemed to plead for its divinity. The sun in the heavens, the mellow lines of upland, the blue mystery of the far plains, were all part of that soft voice. I felt bitter scorn for myself. I was guilty of blood; nay, I was guilty of the sin against light which knows no forgiveness. I was murdering innocent gentleness--and there would be no peace on earth for me. Yet I sat helpless. The power of a sterner will constrained me. And all the while the voice was growing fainter and dying away into unutterable sorrow.

Suddenly a great flame sprang to heaven, and a pall of smoke. I heard men crying out, and fragments of stone fell around the ruins of the grove. When the air cleared, the little tower had gone out of sight.

The voice had ceased and there seemed to me to be a bereaved silence in the world. The shock moved me to my feet, and I ran down the slope to where Jobson stood rubbing his eyes.

"That's done the job. Now we maun get up the tree roots. We've no time to howk. We'll just blast the feck o' them."

The work of destruction went on, but I was coming back to my senses. I forced myself to be practical and reasonable. I thought of the night's experience and Lawson's haggard eyes, and I screwed myself into a determination to see the thing through. I had done the deed; it was my business to make it complete. A text in Jeremiah came into my head:

"Their children remember their altars and their groves by the green trees upon the high hills."

I would see to it that this grove should be utterly forgotten.

We blasted the tree-roots, and, yolking oxen, dragged the debris into a great heap. Then the men set to work with their spades, and roughly levelled the ground. I was getting back to my old self, and Jobson's spirit was becoming mine.

"There is one thing more," I told him "Get ready a couple of ploughs. We will improve upon King Josiah." My brain was a medley of Scripture precedents, and I was determined that no safeguard should be wanting.

We yoked the oxen again and drove the ploughs over the site of the grove. It was rough ploughing, for the place was thick with bits of stone from the tower, but the slow Afrikaner oxen plodded on, and sometime in the afternoon the work was finished. Then I sent down to the farm for bags of rock-salt, such as they use for cattle. Jobson and I took a sack apiece, and walked up and down the furrows, sowing them with salt.

The last act was to set fire to the pile of tree trunks. They burned well, and on the top we flung the bodies of the green doves. The birds of Ashtaroth had an honourable pyre.

THE MOON ENDURETH

Then I dismissed the much-perplexed men, and gravely shook hands with Jobson. Black with dust and smoke I went back to the house, where I bade Travers pack my bags and order the motor. I found Lawson's servant, and heard from him that his master was sleeping peacefully. I gave him some directions, and then went to wash and change.

Before I left I wrote a line to Lawson. I began by transcribing the verses from the 23rd chapter of 2nd Kings. I told him what I had done, and my reason. "I take the whole responsibility upon myself," I wrote. "No man in the place had anything to do with it but me. I acted as I did for the sake of our old friendship, and you will believe it was no easy task for me. I hope you will understand. Whenever you are able to see me send me word, and I will come back and settle with you. But I think you will realise that I have saved your soul."

The afternoon was merging into twilight as I left the house on the road to Taqui. The great fire, where the Grove had been, was still blazing fiercely, and the smoke made a cloud over the upper glen, and filled all the air with a soft violet haze. I knew that I had done well for my friend, and that he would come to his senses and be grateful. My mind was at ease on that score, and in something like comfort I faced the future. But as the car reached the ridge I looked back to the vale I had outraged. The moon was rising and silvering the smoke, and through the gaps I could see the tongues of fire. Somehow, I know not why, the lake, the stream, the garden-coverts, even the green slopes of hill, wore an air of loneliness and desecration. And then my heartache returned, and I knew that I had driven something lovely and adorable from its last refuge on earth.

WOOD MAGIC

(9TH CENTURY.)

I will walk warily in the wise woods on the fringes of eventide, For the covert is full of noises and the stir of nameless things. I have seen in the dusk of the beeches the shapes of the lords that ride, And down in the marish hollow I have heard the lady who sings. And once in an April gleaming I met a maid on the sward, All marble-white and gleaming and tender and wild of eye;-- I, Jehan the hunter, who speak am a grown man, middling hard, But I dreamt a month of the maid, and wept I knew not why.

Down by the edge of the firs, in a coppice of heath and vine, Is an old moss-grown altar, shaded by briar and bloom, Denys, the priest, hath told me 'twas the lord Apollo's shrine In the days ere Christ came down from God to the Virgin's womb. I never go past but I doff my cap and avert my eyes-

(Were Denys to catch me I trow I'd do penance for half a year)-- For once I saw a flame there and the smoke of a sacrifice, And a voice spake out of the thicket that froze my soul with fear.

Wherefore to God the Father, the Son, and the Holy Ghost, Mary the Blessed Mother, and the kindly Saints as well, I will give glory and praise, and them I cherish the most, For they have the keys of Heaven, and save the soul from Hell. But likewise I will spare for the Lord Apollo a grace, And a bow for the lady Venus-as a friend but not as a thrall. 'Tis true they are out of Heaven, but some day they may win the place; For gods are kittle cattle, and a wise man honours them all.

THE RIDING OF NINEMILEBURN
VII

Sim bent over the meal ark and plumbed its contents with his fist. Two feet and more remained: provender--with care--for a month, till he harvested the waterside corn and ground it at Ashkirk mill. He straightened his back better pleased; and, as he moved, the fine dust flew into his throat and set him coughing. He choked back the sound till his face crimsoned.

But the mischief was done. A woman's voice, thin and weary, came from the ben-end. The long man tiptoed awkwardly to her side. "Canny, lass," he crooned. "It's me back frae the hill. There's a mune and a clear sky, and I'll hae the lave under thack and rape the morn. Syne I'm for Ninemileburn, and the coo 'ill be i' the byre by Setterday. Things micht be waur, and we'll warstle through yet. There was mair tint at Flodden."

The last rays of October daylight that filtered through the straw lattice showed a woman's head on the pillow. The face was white and drawn, and the great black eyes--she had been an Oliver out of Megget--were fixed in the long stare of pain. Her voice had the high lilt and the deep undertones of the Forest.

"The bairn 'ill be gone ere ye ken, Sim," she said wearily. "He canna live without milk, and I've nane to gie him. Get the coo back or lose the son I bore ye. If I were my ordinar' I wad hae't in the byre, though I had to kindle Ninemileburn ower Wat's heid."

She turned miserably on her pillow and the babe beside her set up a feeble crying. Sim busied himself with re-lighting the peat fire. He knew too well that he would never see the milk-cow till he took with him the price of his debt or gave a bond on harvested crops. He had had a bad lambing, and the wet summer had soured his shallow lands. The cess to Branksome was due, and he had had no means to pay it. His father's cousin of the Ninemileburn was a brawling fellow, who never lacked beast in byre or corn in bin, and to him he had gone for the loan. But Wat was a hard man, and demanded surety; so the one cow had travelled the six moorland miles and would not return till the bond was cancelled. As well might he try to get water from stone as move Wat by any tale of a sick wife and dying child.

The peat smoke got into his throat and brought on a fresh fit of coughing. The wet year had played havoc with his chest and his lean shoulders shook with the paroxysms. An anxious look at the bed told him that Marion was drowsing, so he slipped to the door.

Outside, as he had said, the sky was clear. From the plashy hillside came the rumour of swollen burns. Then he was aware of a man's voice shouting.

"Sim," it cried, "Sim o' the Cleuch ... Sim." A sturdy figure came down through the scrog of hazel and revealed itself as his neighbour of the Dodhead. Jamie Telfer lived five miles off in Ettrick, but his was the next house to the Cleuch shieling. Telfer was running, and his round red face shone with sweat.

"Dod, man, Sim, ye're hard o' hearing. I was routin' like to wake the deid, and ye never turned your neck. It's the fray I bring ye. Mount and ride to the Carewoodrig. The word's frae Branksome. I've but Ranklehope to raise, and then me and William's Tam will be on the road to join ye."

"Whatna fray?" Sim asked blankly.

"Ninemileburn. Bewcastle's marching. They riped the place at cockcrow, and took twenty-six kye, five horse and a walth o' plenishing. They were seen fordin' Teviot at ten afore noon, but they're gaun round by Ewes Water, for they durstna try the Hermitage Slack. Forbye they move slow, for the bestial's heavy wark to drive. They shut up Wat in the auld peel, and he didna win free till bye midday. Syne he was off to Branksome, and the word frae Branksome is to raise a' Ettrick, Teviotdale, Ale Water, and the Muirs o' Esk. We look to win up wi' the lads long ere they cross Liddel, and that at the speed they gang will be gey an' near sunrise. It's a braw mune for the job."

Jarnie Telfer lay on his face by the burn and lapped up water like a dog. Then without another word he trotted off across the hillside beyond which lay the Ranklehope.

Sim had a fit of coughing and looked stupidly at the sky. Here was the last straw. He was dog-tired, for he had had little sleep the past week. There was no one to leave with Marion, and Marion was too weak to tend herself. The word was from Branksome, and at another time Branksome was to be obeyed. But now the thing was past reason. What use was there for a miserable careworn man to ride among the swank, well-fed lads in the Bewcastle chase? And then he remembered his cow. She would be hirpling with the rest of the Ninemileburn beasts on the road to the Border. The case was more desperate than he had thought. She was gone for ever unless he helped Wat to win her back. And if she went, where was the milk for the child?

He stared hopelessly up at a darkening sky. Then he went to the lean-to where his horse was stalled. The beast was fresh, for it had not been out for two days--a rough Forest shelty with shaggy fetlocks and a mane like a thicket. Sim set his old saddle on it, and went back to the house.

His wife was still asleep, breathing painfully. He put water on the fire to boil, and fetched a handful of meal from the ark. With this he made a dish of gruel, and set it by the bedside. He drew a pitcher of water from the well, for she might be thirsty. Then he banked up the fire and steeked the window. When she woke she would find food and drink, and he would be back before the next darkening. He dared not look at the child.

The shelty shied at a line of firelight from the window, as Sim flung himself wearily on its back. He had got his long ash spear from its place among the rafters, and donned his leather jacket with the iron studs on breast and shoulder. One of the seams gaped. His wife had been mending it when her pains took her.

He had ridden by Commonside and was high on the Caerlanrig before he saw signs of men. The moon swam in a dim dark sky, and the hills were as yellow as corn. The round top of the Wisp made a clear mark to ride by. Sim was a nervous man, and at another time would never have dared to ride alone by the ruined shieling of Chasehope, where folk said a witch had dwelt long ago and the Devil still came in the small hours. But now he was too full of his cares to have room for dread. With his head on his breast he let the shelty take its own road through the mosses.

But on the Caerlanrig he came on a troop of horse. They were a lusty crowd, well-mounted and armed, with iron basnets and corselets that jingled as they rode. Harden's men, he guessed, with young Harden at the head of them. They cried him greeting as he fell in at the tail. "It's Long Sim o' the Cleuch," one said; "he's sib to Wat or he wadna be here. Sim likes his ain fireside better than the 'Bateable Land'."

The companionship of others cheered him. There had been a time, before he brought Marion from Megget, when he was a well kenned figure on the Borders, a good man at weaponshows and a fierce fighter when his blood was up. Those days were long gone; but the gusto of them returned. No man had ever lightlied him without paying scot. He held up his head and forgot his cares and his gaping jackets. In a little they had topped the hill, and were looking down on the young waters of Ewes.

The company grew, as men dropped in from left and right. Sim recognised the wild hair of Charlie of Geddinscleuch, and the square shoulders of Adam of Frodslaw. They passed Mosspaul, a twinkle far down in the glen, and presently came to the long green slope which is called the Carewoodrig, and which makes a pass from Ewes to

Hermitage. To Sim it seemed that an army had encamped on it. Fires had been lit in a howe, and wearied men slept by them. These were the runners, who all day had been warning the dales. By one fire stood the great figure of Wat o' the Ninemileburn, blaspheming to the skies and counting his losses. He had girded on a long sword, and for better precaution had slung an axe on his back. At the sight of young Harden he held his peace. The foray was Branksome's and a Scott must lead.

Dimly and stupidly, for he was very weary, Sim heard word of the enemy. The beasts had travelled slow, and would not cross Liddel till sunrise. Now they were high up on Tarras water, making for Liddel at a ford below the Castletown. There had been no time to warn the Elliots, but the odds were that Lariston and Mangerton would be out by morning.

"Never heed the Elliots," cried young Harden. "We can redd our ain frays, lads. Haste and ride, and we'll hae Geordie Musgrave long ere he wins to the Ritterford, Borrowstonemoss is the bit for us." And with a light Scott laugh he was in the saddle.

They were now in a land of low hills, which made ill-going. A companion gave Sim the news. Bewcastle and five-score men and the Scots four-score and three. "It's waur to haul than to win," said the man. " Ae man can take ten beasts when three 'ill no keep them. There'll be bluidy war on Tarras side ere the nicht's dune."

Sim was feeling his weariness too sore for speech. He remembered that he had tasted no food for fifteen hours. He found his meal-poke and filled his mouth, but the stuff choked him. It only made him cough fiercely, so that Wat o' the Ninemileburn, riding before him, cursed him for a broken-winded fool. Also he was remembering about Marion, lying sick in the darkness twenty miles over the hills.

The moon was clouded, for an east wind was springing up. It was ill riding on the braeface, and Sim and his shelty floundered among the screes. He was wondering how long it would all last. Soon he must fall down and be the scorn of the Border men. The thought put Marion out of his head again. He set his mind on tending his horse and keeping up with his fellows.

Suddenly a whistle from Harden halted the company. A man came running back from the crown of the rig. A whisper went about that Bewcastle was on the far side, in the little glen called the Brunt Burn. The men held their breath, and in the stillness they heard far off the sound of hooves on stones and the heavy breathing of cattle.

It was a noble spot for an ambuscade. The Borderers scattered over the hillside, some riding south to hold the convoy as it came down the glen. Sim's weariness lightened. His blood ran quicker; he remembered that the cow, his child's one hope, was there before him. He found himself next his cousin Wat, who chewed curses in his great beard. When they topped the rig they saw a quarter of a mile below them the men they sought. The cattle were driven in the centre, with horsemen in front and rear and flankers on the braeside.

"Hae at them, lads," cried Wat o' the Ninemileburn, as he dug spurs into his grey horse. From farther down the glen he was answered with a great shout of "Branksome".

Somehow or other Sim and his shelty got down the steep braeface. The next he knew was that the raiders had turned to meet him--to meet him alone, it seemed; the moon had come out again, and their faces showed white in it. The cattle, as the driving ceased, sank down wearily in the moss. A man with an iron ged turned, cursing to receive Wat's sword on his shoulder-bone. A light began to blaze from down the burn--Sim saw the glitter of it out of the corner of an eye--but the men in front were dark figures with white faces.

The Bewcastle lads were stout fellows, well used to hold as well as take. They closed up in line around the beasts, and the moon lit the tops of their spears. Sim brandished his ash-shaft, which had weighed heavily these last hours, and to his surprise found it light. He found his voice, too, and fell a-roaring like Wat.

Before he knew he was among the cattle. Wat had broken the ring, and men were hacking and slipping among the slab sides of the wearied beasts. The shelty came down over the rump of a red bullock, and Sim was sprawling on his face in the trampled grass. He struggled to rise, and some one had him by the throat.

Anger fired his slow brain. He reached out his long arms and grappled a leather jerkin. His nails found a seam and rent it, for he had mighty fingers. Then he was gripping warm flesh, tearing it like a wild beast, and his assailant with a cry slackened his hold. "Whatna wull-cat..." he began, but he got no further. The hoof of Wat's horse came down on his head and brained him. A splatter of blood fell on Sim's face.

The man was half wild. His shelty had broken back for the hill, but his spear lay a yard off. He seized it and got to his feet, to find that Wat had driven the English over the burn. The cattle were losing their weariness in panic, and tossing wild manes among the Scots. It was like a fight in a winter's byre. The glare on the right grew fiercer, and young Harden's voice rose, clear as a bell, above the tumult. He was swearing by the cross of his sword.

On foot, in the old Border way, Sim followed in Wat's wake, into the bog and beyond the burn. He laired to his knees, but he scarcely heeded it. There was a big man before him, a foolish, red-haired fellow, who was making great play with a cudgel. He had shivered two spears and was singing low to himself. Farther off Wat had his axe in hand and was driving the enemy to the brae. There were dead men in the moss. Sim stumbled over a soft body, and a hand caught feebly at his heel. "To me, lads," cried Wat. "Anither birse and we hae them broken."

But something happened. Harden was pushing the van of the raiders up the stream, and a press of them surged in from the right. Wat found himself assailed on his flank, and gave ground. The big man with the cudgel laughed loud and ran down the hill, and the Scots fell back on Sim. Men tripped over him, and as he rose he found the giant above him with his stick in the air.

The blow fell, glancing from the ash-shaft to Sim's side. Something cracked and his left arm hung limp. But the furies of hell had hold of him now. He rolled over, gripped his spear short, and with a swift turn struck upwards. The big man gave a sob and toppled down into a pool of the burn.

Sim struggled to his feet, and saw that the raiders were beginning to hough the cattle One man was driving a red spear into a helpless beast.

It might have been the Cleuch cow. The sight maddened him, and like a destroying angel he was among them. One man he caught full in the throat, and had to set a foot on breast before he could tug the spear out. Then the head shivered on a steel corselet, and Sim played quarterstaff with the shaft. The violence,of his onslaught turned the tide. Those whom Harden drove up were caught in a vice, and squeezed out, wounded and dying and mad with fear, on to the hill above the burn. Both sides were weary men, or there would have been a grim slaughter. As it was, none followed the runners, and every now and again a Scot would drop like a log, not from wounds but from dead weariness.

Harden's flare was dying down. Dawn was breaking and Sim's wild eyes cleared. Here a press of cattle, dazed with fright, and the red and miry heather. Queer black things were curled and stretched athwart it. He noticed a dead man beside him, perhaps of his own slaying. It was a shabby fellow, in a jacket that gaped like Sim's. His face was thin and patient, and his eyes, even in death, looked puzzled and reproachful. He would be one of the plain folk who had to ride, willy-nilly, on bigger men's quarrels. Sim found himself wondering if he, also, had a famished wife and child at home. The fury of the night had gone, and Sim began to sob from utter tiredness.

He slept in what was half a swoon. When he woke the sun was well up in the sky and the Scots were cooking food. His arm irked him, and his head burned like fire. He felt his body and found nothing worse than bruises, and one long shallow scar where his jacket was torn.

A Teviotdale man brought him a cog of brose. Sim stared at it and sickened: he was too far gone for food. Young Harden passed, and looked curiously at him. "Here's a man that has na spared himsel'," he said. "A drop o' French cordial is the thing for you, Sim." And out of a leathern flask he poured a little draught which he bade Sim swallow.

The liquor ran through his veins and lightened the ache of his head. He found strength to rise and look round. Surely they were short of men. If these were all that were left Bewcastle had been well avenged.

Jamie Telfer enlightened him. "When we had gotten the victory, there were some o' the lads thocht that Bewcastle sud pay scot in beasts as weel as men. Sae Wat and a score mair rade off to lowse Geordie Musgrave's kye. The road's clear, and they'll be back ower Liddell by this time. Dod, there'll be walth o' plenishin' at the Ninemileburn."

Sim was cheered by the news. If Wat got back more than his own he might be generous. They were cooking meat round the fire, the flesh of the cattle killed in the fight. He went down to the nearest blaze, and was given a strip of roast which he found he could swallow.

"How many beasts were killed?" he asked incuriously, and was told three. Saugh poles had been set up to hang the skins on. A notion made Sim stagger to his feet and go to inspect them. There could be no mistake. There hung the brindled hide of Marion's cow.

Wat returned in a cloud of glory, driving three-and-twenty English beasts before him--great white fellows that none could match on the Scottish side. He and his lads clamoured for food, so more flesh was roasted, till the burnside smelt like a kitchen. The Scots had found better than cattle, for five big skins of ale bobbed on their saddles. Wat summoned all to come and drink, and Harden, having no fear of reprisals, did not forbid it.

Sim was becoming a man again. He had bathed his bruises and scratches in the burn, and Will o' Phawhope, who had skill as a leech, had set his arm and bound it to his side in splints of ash and raw hide. He had eaten grossly of flesh--the first time since the spring, and then it had only been braxy lamb. The ale had warmed his blood and quickened his wits. He began to feel pleased with himself. He had done well in the fray--had not young Harden praised him?--and surly Wat had owned that the salvage of so many beasts was Sim's doing. "Man, Sim, ye wrocht michtily at the burnside," he had said. "The heids crackit like nits when ye garred your staff sing. Better you wi' a stick than anither tnan wi' a sword." It was fine praise, and warmed Sim's chilly soul. For a year he had fought bitterly for bread, and now glory had come to him without asking.

Men were drawn by lot to drive the cattle, and others to form a rearguard. The rest set off for their homes by the nearest road. The shelty had been recovered, and Sim to his pride found himself riding in the front with Wat and young Harden and others of the Scott and Elliot gentry.

The company rode fast over the green hills in the clear autumn noon. Harden's blue eyes danced, and he sang snatches in his gay voice. Wat rumbled his own praises and told of the raid over Liddel. Sim felt a new being from the broken man who the night before had wearily jogged on the same road. He told himself he took life too gravely and let care ride him too hard. He was too much thirled to the Cleuch and tied to his wife's apron. In the future he would see his friends, and bend the bicker with the rest of them.

By the darkening they had come to Ninemileburn, where Harden's road left theirs. Wat had them all into the bare dwelling, and another skin of ale was broached. A fire was lit and the men sprawled around it, singing songs. Then tales began, and they would have sat till morning, had not Harden called them to the road. Sim, too, got to his feet. He was thinking of the six miles yet before him, and as home grew nearer his spirits sank. Dimly he remembered the sad things that waited his homecoming.

Wat made him a parting speech. "Gude e'en to ye, Cousin Sim. Ye've been a kind man to me the day. May I do as weel by you if ever the fray gangs by the Cleuch. I had a coo o' yours in pledge, and it was ane o the beasts the Musgraves speared. By the auld law your debt still stands, and if I likit I could seek anither pledge. But there'll be something awin' for rescue-shot, and wi' that and the gude wark ye've dune the day, I'm content to ca' the debt paid."

Wat's words sounded kind, and no doubt Wat thought himself generous. Sim had it on his tongue to ask for a cow--even on a month's loan. But pride choked his speech. It meant telling of the pitiful straits at the Cleuch. After what had passed he must hold his head high amongst those full-fed Branksome lads. He thanked Wat, cried farewell to the rest, and mounted his shelty.

The moon was rising and the hills were yellow as corn. The shelty had had a feed of oats, and capered at the shadows. What with excitement, meat and ale, and the dregs of a great fatigue, Sim's mind was hazy, and his cheerfulness returned. He thought only on his exploits. He had done great things--he, Sim o' the Cleuch--and every man in the Forest would hear of them and praise his courage. There would be ballads made about him; he could hear the blind violer at the Ashkirk change-house singing-- songs which told how Sim o' the Cleuch smote Bewcastle in the howe of the Brunt Burn--ash against steel, one against ten. The fancy intoxicated him; he felt as if he, too, could make a ballad. It would speak of the soft shiny night with the moon high in the heavens. It would tell of the press of men and beasts by the burnside, and the red glare of Harden's fires, and Wat with his axe, and above all of Sim with his ash-shaft and his long arms, and how Harden drove the raiders up the burn and Sim smote them silently among the cattle. Wat's exploits would come in, but the true glory was Sim's. But for him Scots saddles might have been empty and every beast safe over Liddel.

The picture fairly ravished him. It carried him over the six miles of bent and down by the wood of hazel to where the Cleuch lay huddled in its nook of hill. It brought him to the door of his own silent dwelling. As he pushed into the darkness his heart suddenly sank...

With fumbling hands he kindled a rushlight. The peat fire had long gone out and left only a heap of white ashes. The gruel by the bed had been spilled and was lying on the floor. Only the jug of water was drained to the foot.

His wife lay so still that he wondered. A red spot burned in each cheek, and, as he bent down, he could hear her fast breathing. He flashed the light on her eyes and she slowly opened them.

"The coo, Sim," she said faintly. "Hae ye brocht the coo?"

The rushlight dropped on the floor. Now he knew the price of his riding. He fell into a fit of coughing.

PLAIN FOLK

Since flaming angels drove our sire From Eden's green to walk the mire, We are the folk who tilled the plot And ground the grain and boiled the pot. We hung the garden terraces That pleasured Queen Semiramis. Our toil it was and burdened brain That set the Pyramids o'er the plain. We marched from Egypt at God's call And drilled the ranks and fed them all; But never Eschol's wine drank we,-- Our bones lay 'twixt the sand

and sea. We officered the brazen bands That rode the far and desert lands; We bore the Roman eagles forth And made great roads from south to north; White cities flowered for holidays, But we, forgot, died far away. And when the Lord called folk to Him, And some sat blissful at His feet, Ours was the task the bowl to brim, For on this earth even saints must eat. The serfs have little need to think, Only to work and sleep and drink; A rover's life is boyish play, For when cares press he rides away; The king sits on his ruby throne, And calls the whole wide world his own. But we, the plain folk, noon and night No surcease of our toil we see; We cannot ease our cares by flight, For Fortune holds our loves in fee. We are not slaves to sell our wills, We are not kings to ride the hills, But patient men who jog and dance In the dull wake of circumstance; Loving our little patch of sun, Too weak our homely dues to shun, Too nice of conscience, or too free, To prate of rights--if rights there be.

The Scriptures tell us that the meek The earth shall have to work their will; It may be they shall find who seek, When they have topped the last long hill. Meantime we serve among the dust For at the best a broken crust, A word of praise, and now and then The joy of turning home again. But freemen still we fall or stand, We serve because our hearts command. Though kings may boast and knights cavort, We broke the spears at Agincourt. When odds were wild and hopes were down, We died in droves by Leipsic town. Never a field was starkly won But ours the dead that faced the sun. The slave will fight because he must, The rover for his ire and lust, The king to pass an idle hour Or feast his fatted heart with power; But we, because we choose, we choose, Nothing to gain and much to lose, Holding it happier far to die Than falter in our decency.

The serfs may know an hour of pride When the high flames of tumult ride. The rover has his days of ease When he has sacked his palaces. A king may live a year like God When prostrate peoples drape the sod. We ask for little,-leave to tend Our modest fields: at daylight's end The fires of home: a wife's caress: The star of children's happiness. Vain hope! 'Tis ours for ever and aye To do the job the slaves have marred, To clear the wreckage of the fray, And please our kings by working hard. Daily we mend their blunderings, Swachbucklers, demagogues, and kings!

What if we rose?-If some fine morn, Unnumbered as the autumn corn, With all the brains and all the skill Of stubborn back and steadfast will, We rose and, with the guns in train, Proposed to deal the cards again, And, tired of sitting up o' nights, Gave notice to our parasites, Announcing that in future they Who paid the piper should call the lay! Then crowns would tumble down like nuts, And wastrels hide in water-butts; Each lamp-post as an epilogue: Would hold a pendent demagogue: Then would the world be for the wise!--

. . . .

But ah! the plain folk never rise.

THE KINGS OF ORION
VIII

" An ape and a lion lie side by side in the heart of a man."

--PERSIAN PROVERB

Spring-fishing in the North is a cold game for a man whose blood has become thin in gentler climates. All afternoon I had failed to stir a fish, and the wan streams of the Laver, swirling between bare grey banks, were as icy to the eye as the sharp gusts of hail from the north-east were to the fingers. I cast mechanically till I grew weary, and then with an empty creel and a villainous temper set myself to trudge the two miles of bent to the inn. Some distant ridges of hill stood out snow-clad against the dun sky, and half in anger, half in dismal satisfaction, I told myself that fishing to-morrow would be as barren as to-day.

At the inn door a tall man was stamping his feet and watching a servant lifting rodcases from a dog-cart. Hooded and wrapped though he was, my friend Thirlstone was an unmistakable figure in any landscape. The long, haggard, brown face, with the skin drawn tightly over the cheek-bones, the keen blue eyes finely wrinkled round the corners with staring at many suns, the scar which gave his mouth a humorous droop to the right, made up a whole which was not easily forgotten. I had last seen him on the quay at Funchal bargaining with some rascally boatman to take him after mythical wild goats in Las Desertas. Before that we had met at an embassy ball in Vienna, and still earlier at a hill-station in Persia to which I had been sent post-haste by an anxious and embarrassed Government. Also I had been at school with him, in those far-away days when we rode nine stone and dreamed of cricket averages. He was a soldier of note, who had taken part in two little wars and one big one; had himself conducted a political mission through a hard country with some success, and was habitually chosen by his superiors to keep his eyes open as a foreign attache in our neighbours' wars. But his fame as a hunter had gone abroad into places where even the name of the British army is unknown. He was the hungriest shikari I have ever seen, and I have seen many. If you are wise you will go forthwith to some library and procure a little book entitled "Three Hunting Expeditions," by A.W.T. It is a modest work, and the style is that of a leading article, but all the lore and passion of the Red Gods are in its pages.

The sitting-room at the inn is a place of comfort, and while Thirlstone warmed his long back at the fire I sank contentedly into one of the well-rubbed leather arm-chairs. The company of a friend made the weather and scarcity of salmon less the intolerable grievance they had seemed an hour ago than a joke to be laughed at. The landlord came in with whisky, and banked up the peats till they glowed beneath a pall of blue smoke.

"I hope to goodness we are alone," said Thirlstone, and he turned to the retreating landlord and asked the question.

"There's naebody bidin' the nicht forbye yoursels," he said, "but the morn there's a gentleman comin'. I got a letter frae him the day. Maister Wiston, they ca him. Maybe ye ken him?"

I started at the name, which I knew very well. Thirlstone, who knew it better, stopped warming himself and walked to the window, where he stood pulling his moustache and staring at the snow. When the man had left the room, he turned to me with the face of one whose mind is made up on a course but uncertain of the best method.

"Do you know this sort of weather looks infernally unpromising? I've half a mind to chuck it and go back to town."

I gave him no encouragement, finding amusement in his difficulties. "Oh, it's not so bad," I said, "and it won't last. To-morrow we may have the day of our lives."

He was silent for a little, staring at the fire. "Anyhow," he said at last, "we were fools to be so far up the valley. Why shouldn't we go down to the Forest Lodge? They'll take us in, and we should be deucedly comfortable, and the water's better."

"There's not a pool on the river to touch the stretch here," I said. "I know, for I've fished every inch of it."

He had no reply to this, so he lit a pipe and held his peace for a time. Then, with some embarrassment but the air of having made a discovery, he announced that his conscience was troubling him about his work, and he thought he ought to get back to it at once. "There are several things I have forgotten to see to, and they're rather important. I feel a beast behaving like this, but you won't mind, will you?"

"My dear Thirlstone," I said, "what is the good of hedging? Why can't you say you won't meet Wiston!"

His face cleared. "Well, that's the fact--I won't. It would be too infernally unpleasant. You see, I was once by way of being his friend, and he was in my regiment. I couldn't do it."

The landlord came in at the moment with a basket of peats. "How long is Capt.--Mr. Wiston staying here?" I asked.

"He's no bidin' ony time. He's just comin' here in the middle o' the day for his denner, and then drivin' up the water to Altbreac. He has the fishin' there."

Thirlstone's face showed profound relief. "Thank God!" I heard him mutter under his breath, and when the landlord had gone he fell to talking of salmon with enthusiasm. "We must make a big day of it to-morrow, dark to dark, you know. Thank Heaven, our beat's down-stream, too." And thereafter he made frequent excursions to the door, and bulletins on the weather were issued regularly.

Dinner over, we drew our chairs to the hearth, and fell to talk and the slow consumption of tobacco. When two men from the ends of the earth meet by a winter fire, their thoughts are certain to drift overseas. We spoke of the racing tides off Vancouver, and the lonely pine-clad ridges running up to the snow-peaks of the Selkirks, to which we had both travelled once upon a time in search of sport. Thirlstone on his own account had gone wandering to Alaska, and brought back some bear-skins and a frost-bitten toe as trophies, and from his tales had consorted with the finest band of rogues which survives unhanged on this planet. Then some casual word took our thoughts to the south, and our memories dallied with Africa. Thirlstone had hunted in Somaliland and done mighty slaughter; while I had spent some never-to-be forgotten weeks long ago in the hinterland of Zanzibar, in the days before railways and game-preserves. I have gone through life with a keen eye for the discovery of earthly paradises, to which I intend to retire when my work is over, and the fairest I thought I had found above the Rift valley, where you had a hundred miles of blue horizon and the weather of Scotland. Thirlstone, not having been there, naturally differed, and urged the claim of a certain glen in Kashmir, where you may hunt two varieties of bear and three of buck in thickets of rhododendron, and see the mightiest mountain-wall on earth from your tent door. The mention of the Indian frontier brought us back to our professions, and for a little we talked "shop" with the unblushing confidence of those who know each other's work and approve it. As a very young soldier Thirlstone had gone shooting in the Pamirs, and had blundered into a Russian party of exploration which contained Kuropatkin. He had in consequence grossly outstayed his leave, having been detained for a fortnight by an arbitrary hospitality; but he had learned many things, and the experience had given him strong views on frontier questions. Half an hour was devoted to a masterly survey of the East, until a word pulled us up.

"I went there in '99" Thirlstone was saying,--"the time Wiston and I were sent--" and then he stopped, and his eager face clouded. Wiston's name cast a shadow over our reminiscences.

"What did he actually do?" I asked after a short silence.

"Pretty bad! He seemed a commonplace, good sort of fellow, popular, fairly competent, a little bad-tempered perhaps. And then suddenly he did something so extremely blackguardly that everything was at an end. It's no good repeating details, and I hate to think about it. We know little about our neighbours, and I'm not so sure that we know much about ourselves. There may be appalling depths of iniquity in every one of us, only most people are fortunate enough to go through the world without meeting anything to wake the devil in them. I don't believe Wiston was bad in the ordinary sense. Only there was something else in him--somebody else, if you like--and in a moment it came uppermost, and he was a branded man. Ugh! it's a gruesome thought." Thirlstone had let his pipe go out, and was staring moodily into the fire.

"How do you explain things like that?" he asked. "I have an idea of my own about them. We talk glibly of ourselves and our personality and our conscience, as if every man's nature were a smooth, round, white thing, like a chuckie-stone. But I believe there are two men-perhaps more-in every one of us. There's our ordinary self, generally rather humdrum; and then there's a bit of something else, good, bad, but never indifferent,--and it is that something else which may make a man a saint or a great villain."

"'The Kings of Orion have come to earth,'" I quoted.

Something in the words struck Thirlstone, and he asked me what was the yarn I spoke of.

"It's an old legend," I explained. "When the kings were driven out of Orion, they were sent to this planet and given each his habitation in some mortal soul. There were differences of character in that royal family, and so the alter ego which dwells alongside of us may be virtuous or very much the reverse. But the point is that he is always greater than ourselves, for he has been a king. It's a foolish story, but very widely believed. There is something oi the sort in Celtic folk-lore, and there's a reference to it in Ausonius. Also the bandits in the Bakhtiari have a version of it in a very excellent ballad."

"Kings of Orion," said Thirlstone musingly. "I like that idea. Good or bad, but always great! After all, we show a kind of belief in it in our daily practice. Every man is always making fancies about himself; but it is never his workaday self, but something else. The bank clerk who pictures himself as a financial Napoleon knows that his own thin little soul is incapable of it; but he knows, too, that it is possible enough for that other bigger thing which is not his soul, but yet in some odd way is bound up with it. I fancy myself a field-marshal in a European war; but I know perfectly well that if the job were offered me, I should realise my incompetence and decline. I expect you rather picture yourself now and then as a sort of Julius Caesar and empire-maker, and yet, with all respect, my dear chap, I think it would be rather too much for you."

"There was once a man," I said, "an early Victorian Whig, whose chief ambitions were to reform the criminal law and abolish slavery. Well, this dull, estimable man in his leisure moments was Emperor of Byzantium. He fought great wars and built palaces, and then, when the time for fancy was past, went into the House of Commons and railed against militarism and Tory extravagance. That particular king from Orion had a rather odd sort of earthly tenement."

Thirlstone was all interest. "A philosophic Whig and the throne of Byzantium. A pretty rum mixture! And yet--yet," and his eyes became abstracted. "Did you ever know Tommy Lacelles?"

"The man who once governed Deira? Retired now, and lives somewhere in Kent. Yes, I've met him once or twice. But why?"

"Because," said Thirlstone solemnly, " nless I'm greatly mistaken, Tommy was another such case, though no man ever guessed it except myself. I don't mind telling you the story, now that he is retired and vegetating in his ancestral pastures. Besides, the facts are all in his favour, and the explanation is our own business....

"His wife was my cousin, and when she died Tommy was left a very withered, disconsolate man, with no particular object in life. We all thought he would give up the service, for he was hideously well off and then one fine day, to our amazement, he was offered Deira, and accepted it. I was short of a job at the time, for my battalion was at home, and there was nothing going on anywhere, so I thought I should like to see what the East Coast of Africa was like, and wrote to Tommy about it. He jumped at me, cabled offering me what he called his Military Secretaryship, and I got seconded, and set off. I had never known him very well, but what I had seen I had liked; and I suppose he was glad to have one of Maggie's family with him, for he was still very low about her loss. I was in pretty good spirits, for it meant new experiences, and I had hopes of big game.

"You've never been to Deira? Well, there's no good trying to describe it, for it's the only place in the world like itself. God made it and left it to its own devices. The town is pretty enough, with its palms and green headland, and little scrubby islands in the river's mouth. It has the usual half-Arab, half-Portugee look-white green-shuttered houses, flat roofs, sallow little men in duck, and every type of nigger from the Somali to the Shangaan. There are some good buildings, and Government House was the mansion of some old Portugee seigneur, and was built when people in Africa were not in such a hurry as to-day. Inland there's a rolling, forest country, beginning with decent trees and ending in mimosa-thorn, when the land begins to rise to the stony hills of the interior; and that poisonous yellow river rolls through it all, with a denser native population along its banks than you will find anywhere else north of the Zambesi. For about two months in the year the climate is Paradise, and for the rest you live in a Turkish bath, with every known kind of fever hanging about. We cleaned out the town and improved the sanitation, so there were few epidemics, but there was enough ordinary malaria to sicken a crocodile.

"The place was no special use to us. It had been annexed in spite of a tremendous Radical outcry, and, upon my soul, it was one of the few cases where the Radicals had something to say for themselves. All we got by it was half a dozen of the nastiest problems an unfortunate governor can have to face. Ten years before it had been a decaying strip of coast, with a few trading firms in the town, and a small export of ivory and timber. But some years before Tommy took it up there had been a huge discovery of copper in the hills inland, a railway had been built, and there were several biggish mining settlements at the end of it. Deira itself was filled with offices of European firms, it had got a Stock Exchange of its own, and it was becoming the usual cosmopolitan playground. It had a knack, too, of getting the very worst breed of adventurer. I know something of your South African and Australian mining town, and with all their faults they are run by white men. If they haven't much morals, they have a kind of decency which keeps them fairly straight. But for our sins we got a brand of Levantine Jew, who was fit for nothing but making money and making trouble. They were always defying the law, and then, when they got into a hole, they squealed to Government for help, and started a racket in the home papers about the weakness of the Imperial power. The crux of the whole difficulty was the natives, who lived along the river and in the foothills. They were a hardy race of Kaffirs, sort of far-away cousins to the Zulu, and till the mines were opened they had behaved well enough. They had arms, which we had never dared to take away, but they kept quiet and paid their hut-taxes like men. I got to know many of the chiefs, and liked them, for they were upstanding fellows to look at and heavenborn shikaris. However, when the Jews came along they wanted labour, and, since we did not see our way to allow them to add to the imported coolie population, they had to fall back upon the Labonga. At first things went smoothly. The chiefs were willing to let their men work for good wages, and for a time there was enough labour for everybody. But as the mines extended, and the natives, after making a few pounds, wanted to get back to their kraals, there came a shortage; and since the work could not be allowed to slacken, the owners tried other methods. They made promises which they never intended to keep, and they stood on the letter of a law which the natives did not understand, and they employed touts who were little better than slave-dealers. They got the labour, of course, but soon they had put the Labonga into a state of unrest which a very little would turn into a rising.

"Into this kettle of fish Tommy was pitchforked, and when I arrived he was just beginning to understand how unpleasant it was. As I said before, I did not know him very well, and I was amazed to find how bad he was at his job. A more curiously incompetent person I never met. He was a long, thin man, with a grizzled moustache and a mild sleepy eye- not an impressive figure, except on a horse; and he had an odd lisp which made even a shrewd remark sound foolish. He was the most industrious creature in the world, and a model of official decorum. His papers were always in order, his despatches always neat and correct, and I don't believe any one ever caught him tripping in office work. But he had no more conception than a child of the kind of trouble that was brewing. He knew never an honest man from a rogue, and the result was that he received all unofficial communications with a polite disbelief. I used to force him to see people-miners, prospectors, traders, any one who had something to say worth listening to, but it all glided smoothly off his mind. He was simply the most incompetent being ever created, living in the world as not being of it, or rather creating a little official world of his own, where all events happened on lines laid down by the Colonial Office, and men were like papers, to be rolled into packets and properly docketed. He had an Executive Council of people like himself, competent officials and blind bats at anything else. Then there was a precious Legislative Council, intended to represent the different classes of the population. There were several good men on it-one old trader called Mackay, for instance, who had been thirty years in the country-but most were nominees of the mining firms, and very seedy rascals at that. They were always talking about the rights of the white man, and demanding popular control of the Government, and similar twaddle. The leader was a man who hailed from Hamburg, and called himself Le Foy--descended from a Crusader of the name of Levi--who was a jackal of one of the chief copper firms. He overflowed with Imperialist sentiment, and when he wasn't waving the flag he used to gush about the beauties of English country life the grandeur of the English tradition. He hated me from the start, for when he talked of going 'home' I thought he meant Hamburg, and said so; and then a thing happened which made him hate me worse. He was infernally rude to Tommy, who, like the dear sheep he was, never saw it, and, if he had, wouldn't have minded. But one day I chanced to overhear some of his impertinences, so I hunted out my biggest sjambok and lay in wait for Mr. Le Foy. I told him that he was a representative of the sovereign people, that I was a member of an effete bureaucracy, and that it would be most painful if unpleasantness arose between us. But, I added, I was prepared, if necessary, to sacrifice my official career to my private feelings, and if he dared to use such language again to his Majesty's representative I would give him a hiding he would remember till he found himself in Abraham's bosom. Not liking my sjambok, he became soap and butter at once, and held his tongue for a month or two.

"But though Tommy was no good at his job, he was a tremendous swell at' other things. He was an uncommonly good linguist, and had always about a dozen hobbies which he slaved at; and when he found himself at

Deira with a good deal of leisure, he became a bigger crank than ever. He had a lot of books which used to follow him about the world in zinc-lined boxes--your big paper-backed German books which mean research,--and he was a Fellow of the Koyal Society, and corresponded with half a dozen foreign shows. India was his great subject, but he had been in the Sudan and knew a good deal about African races. When I went out to him, his pet hobby was the Bantu, and he had acquired an amazing amount of miscellaneous learning. He knew all about their immigration from the North, and the Arab and Phoenician trade-routes, and the Portuguese occupation, and the rest of the history of that unpromising seaboard. The way he behaved in his researches showed the man. He worked hard at the Labonga language-which, I believe, is a linguistic curiosity of the first water-from missionary books and the conversation of tame Kaffirs. But he never thought of paying them a visit in their native haunts. I was constantly begging him to do it, but it was not Tommy's way. He did not care a straw about political experience, and he liked to look at things through the medium of paper and ink. Then there were the Phoenician remains in the foot-hills where the copper was mined-old workings, and things which might have been forts or temples. He knew all that was to be known about them, but he had never seen them and never wanted to. Once only he went to the hills, to open some new reservoirs and make the ordinary Governor's speech; but he went in a special train and stayed two hours, most of which was spent in lunching and being played to by brass bands.

"But, oddly enough, there was one thing which stirred him with an interest that was not academic. I discovered it by accident one day when I went into his study and found him struggling with a map of Central Asia. Instead of the mild, benevolent smile with which he usually greeted my interruptions, he looked positively furtive, and, I could have sworn, tried to shuffle the map under some papers. Now it happens that Central Asia is the part of the globe that I know better than most men, and I could not help picking up the map and looking at it. It was a wretched thing, and had got the Oxus two hundred miles out of its course. I pointed this out to Tommy, and to my amazement he became quite excited. 'Nonsense,' he said. 'You don't mean to say it goes south of that desert. Why, I meant to--,' and then he stammered and stopped. I wondered what on earth he had meant to do, but I merely observed that I had been there, and knew. That brought Tommy out of his chair in real excitement. 'What!' he cried, 'you! You never told me,' and he started to fire off a round of questions, which showed that if he knew very little about the place, he had it a good deal in his mind.

I drew some sketch-plans for him, and left him brooding over them.

"That was the first hint I got. The second was a few nights later, when we were smoking in the billiard-room. I had been reading Marco Polo, and the talk got on to Persia and drifted all over the north side of the Himalaya. Tommy, with an abstracted eye, talked of Alexander and Timour and Genghis Khan, and particularly of Prester John, who was a character and took his fancy. I had told him that the natives in the Pamirs were true Persian stock, and this interested him greatly. 'Why was there never a great state built up in those valleys?' he asked. 'You get nothing but a few wild conquerors rushing east and west, and then some squalid khanates. And yet all the materials were there--the stuff for a strong race, a rich land, the traditions of an old civilisation, and natural barriers against all invasion.'

"'I suppose they never found the man,' I said.

"He agreed. 'Their princes were sots, or they were barbarians of genius who could devastate to the gates of Peking or Constantinople, but could never build. They did not recognise their limits, and so they went out in a whirlwind. But if there had been a man of solid genius he might have built up the strongest nation on the globe. In time he could have annexed Persia and nibbled at China. He would have been rich, for he could tap all the inland trade-routes of Asia. He would have had to be a conqueror, for his people would be a race of warriors, but first and foremost he must have been a statesman. Think of such a civilisation, THE Asian civilisation, growing up mysteriously behind the deserts and the ranges! That's my idea of Prester John. Russia would have been confined to the line of the Urals. China would have been absorbed. There would have been no Japan. The whole history of the world for the last few hundred years would have been different. It is the greatest of all the lost chances in history.' Tommy waxed pathetic over the loss.

"I was a little surprised at his eloquence, especially when he seemed to remember himself and stopped all of a sudden. But for the next week I got no peace with his questions. I told him all I knew of Bokhara, and Samarkand, and Tashkend, and Yarkand. I showed him the passes in the Pamirs and the Hindu Kush. I traced out the rivers, and I calculated distances; we talked over imaginary campaigns, and set up fanciful constitutions. It a was childish game, but I found it interesting enough. He spoke of it all with a curious personal tone which puzzled me, till one day when we were amusing ourselves with a fight on the Zarafshan, and I put in a modest claim to be allowed to win once in a while. For a second he looked at me in blank surprise. 'You can't,' he said; 'I've got to enter Samarkand before I can...' and he stopped again, with a glimmering sense in his face that he was giving himself away. And then I knew that I had surprised Tommy's secret. While he was muddling his own job, he was salving his pride with fancies of some wild career in Asia, where Tommy, disguised as the lord knows what Mussulman grandee, was hammering the little states into an empire.

"I did not think then as I think now, and I was amused to find so odd a trait in a dull man. I had known something of the kind before. I had met fellows who after their tenth peg would begin to swagger about some ridiculous fancy of their own--their little private corner of soul showing for a moment when the drink had blown aside their common-sense. Now, I had never known the thing appear in cold blood and everyday life, but I assumed the case to be the same. I thought of it only as a harmless fancy, never imagining that it had anything to do with character. I put it down to that kindly imagination which is the old opiate for failures. So I played up to Tommy with all my might, and though he became very discreet after the first betrayal, having hit upon the clue, I knew what to look for, and I found it. When I told him that the Labonga were in a devil of a mess, he would look at me with an empty face and change the subject; but once among the Turcomans his eye would kindle, and he would slave at his confounded folly with sufficient energy to reform the whole East Coast. It was the spark that kept the man alive. Otherwise he would have been as limp as a rag, but this craziness put life into him, and made him carry his head in the air and walk like a free man. I remember he was very keen about any kind of martial poetry. He used to go about crooning Scott and Macaulay to himself, and when we went for a walk or a ride he wouldn't speak for miles, but keep smiling to himself and humming bits of songs. I daresay he was very happy,--far happier than your stolid, competent man, who sees only the one thing to do and does it. Tommy was muddling his particular duty, but building glorious palaces in the air.

"One day Mackay, the old trader, came to me after a sitting of the precious Legislative Council. We were very friendly, and I had done all I could to get the Government to listen to his views. He was a dour, ill-tempered Scotsman, very anxious for the safety of his property, but perfectly careless about any danger to himself.

"'Captain Thirlstone,' he said, 'that Governor of yours is a damned fool.'

"Of course I shut him up very brusquely, but he paid no attention. 'He just sits and grins, and lets yon Pentecostal crowd we've gotten here as a judgment for our sins do what they like wi' him. God kens what'll happen. I would go home to-morrow, if I could realise without an immoderate loss. For the day of reckoning is at hand. Maark my words, Captain--at hand.'

"I said I agreed with him about the approach of trouble, but that the Governor would rise to the occasion. I told him that people like Tommy were only seen at their best in a crisis, and that he might be perfectly confident that when it arrived he would get a new idea of the man. I said this, but of course I did not believe a word of it. I thought Tommy was only a dreamer, who had rotted any grit he ever possessed by his mental opiates. At that time I did not understand about the kings from Orion.

" And then came the thing we had all been waiting for--a Labonga rising. A week before I had got leave and had gone up country, partly to shoot, but mainly to see for myself what trouble was brewing. I kept away from the river, and therefore missed the main native centres, but such kraals as I passed had a look I did not like. The chiefs were almost always invisible, and the young bloods were swaggering about and bukking to each other, while the women were grinding maize as if for some big festival. However, after a bit the country seemed to grow more normal, and I went into the foothills to shoot, fairly easy in my mind. I had got up to a place called Shimonwe, on the Pathi river, where I had ordered letters to be sent, and one night coming in from a hard day after kudu I found a post-runner half-dead of fatigue with a chit from Utterson, who commanded a police district twenty miles nearer the coast. It said simply that all the young men round about him had cleared out and appeared to be moving towards Deira, that he was in the devil of a quandary, and that, since the police were under the Governor, he would take his orders from me.

"It looked as if the heather were fairly on fire at last, so I set off early next morning to trek back. About midday I met Utterson, a very badly scared little man, who had come to look for me. It seemed that his policemen had bolted in the night and gone to join the rising, leaving him with two white sergeants, barely fifty rounds of ammunition, and no neighbour for a hundred miles. He said that the Labonga chiefs were not marching to the coast, as he had thought, but north along the eastern foothills in the direction of the mines. This was better news, for it meant that in all probability the railway would remain open. It was my business to get somehow to my chief, and I was in the deuce of a stew how to manage it. It was no good following the line of the natives' march, for they would have been between me and my goal, and the only way was to try and outflank them by going due east, in the Deira direction, and then turning north, so as to strike the railway about half-way to the mines. I told Utterson we had better scatter, otherwise we should have no chance of getting through a densely populated native country. So, about five in the afternoon I set off with my chief shikari, who, by good luck, was not a Labonga, and dived into the jungly bush which skirts the hills.

"For three days I had a baddish time. We steered by the stars, travelling chiefly by night, and we showed extraordinary skill in missing the water-holes. I had a touch of fever and got light-headed, and it was all I could do to struggle through the thick grass and wait-a-bit thorns. My clothes were torn to rags, and I grew so footsore that it was agony to move. All the same we travelled fast, and there was no chance of our missing the road, for any route due north was bound to cut the railway. I had the most sickening uncertainty about what was to come next. Hely, who was in command at Deira, was a good enough man, but he had only three companies of white troops, and the black troops were as likely as not to be on their way to the rebels. It looked as if we should have a Cawnpore business on a small scale, though I thanked Heaven there were no women in the case. As for Tommy, he would probably be repeating platitudes in Deira and composing an intelligent despatch on the whole subject.

"About four in the afternoon of the third day I struck the line near a little station called Palala. I saw by the look of the rails that trains were still running, and my hopes revived. At Palala there was a coolie stationmaster, who gave me a drink and a little food, after which I slept heavily in his office till wakened by the arrival of an up train. It contained one of the white companies and a man Davidson, of the 101st, who was Hely's second in command. From him I had news that took away my breath. The Governor had gone up the line two days before with an A.D.C. and old Mackay. 'The sportsman has got a move on him at last,' said Davidson, 'but what he means to do Heaven only knows. The Labonga are at the mines, and a kind of mine-guard has been formed for defence. The joke of it is that most of the magnates are treed up there, for the railway is cut and they can't get away. I don't envy your chief the job of schooling that nervous crowd.'

"I went on with Davidson, and very early next morning we came to a broken culvert and had to stop. There we stuck for three hours till the down train arrived, and with it Hely. He was for ordinary a stolid soul, but I never saw a man in such a fever of excitement. He gripped me by the arm and fairly shook me. 'That old man of yours is a hero,' he cried. 'The Lord forgive me! and I have always crabbed him.'

"I implored him in Heaven's name to tell me what was up, but he would say nothing till he had had his pow-pow with Davidson. It seemed that he was bringing all his white troops up the line for some great demonstration that Tommy had conceived. Davidson went back to Deira, while we mended the culvert and got the men transferred to the other train. Then I screwed the truth out of Hely. Tommy had got up to the mines before the rebels arrived, and had found as fine a chaos as can be imagined. He did not seem to have had any doubts what to do. There was a certain number of white workmen, hard fellows from Cornwall mostly, with a few Australians, and these he got together with Mackay's help and organised into a pretty useful corps. He set them to guard the offices, and gave them strict orders to shoot at sight any one attempting to leave. Then he collected the bosses and talked to them like a father. What he said Hely did not know, except that he had damned their eyes pretty heartily, and told them what a set of swine they were, making trouble which they had not the pluck to face. Whether from Mackay, or from his own intelligence, or from a memory of my neglected warnings, he seemed to have got a tight grip on the facts at last. Meanwhile, the Labonga were at the doors, chanting their battle-songs half a mile away, and shots were heard from the far pickets. If they had tried to rush the place then, all would have been over, but, luckily, that was never their way of fighting. They sat down in camp to make their sacrifices and consult their witch-doctors, and presently Hely arrived with the first troops, having come in on the northern flank when he found the line cut. He had been in time to hear the tail-end of Tommy's final address to the mineowners. He told them, in words which Hely said he could never have imagined coming from his lips, that they would be well served if the Labonga cleaned the whole place out. Only, he said, that would be against the will of Britain, and it was his business, as a loyal servant, to prevent it. Then, after giving Hely his instructions, he had put on his uniform, gold lace and all, and every scrap of bunting he possessed--all the orders and 'Golden Stars' of half a dozen Oriental States where he had served. He made Ashurst, the A.D.C., put on his best Hussar's kit, and Mackay rigged himself out in a frock-coat and a topper; and the three set out on horseback for the Labonga. 'I believe he'll bring it off,' said Hely, with wild eyes,n'and, by Heaven, if he does, it'll be the best thing since John Nicholson!'

"For the rest of the way I sat hugging myself with excitement. The miracle of miracles seemed to have come. The old, slack, incompetent soul in Tommy seemed to have been driven out by that other spirit, which had hitherto been content to dream of crazy victories on the Oxus. I cursed my folly in having missed it all, for I would have given my right hand to be with him among the Labonga. I envied that young fool

Ashurst his luck in being present at that queer transformation scene. I had not a doubt that Tommy would bring it off all right. The kings from Orion don't go into action without coming out on top. As we got near the mines I kept my ears open for the sound of shots; but all was still,--not even the kind of hubbub a native force makes when it is on the move. Something had happened, but what it was no man could guess. When we got to where the line was up, we made very good time over the five miles to the mines. No one interfered with us, and the nearer we got the greater grew my certainty. Soon we were at the pickets, who had nothing to tell us; and then we were racing up the long sandy street to the offices, and there, sitting smoking on the doorstep of the hotel, surrounded by everybody who was not on duty, were Mackay and Ashurst.

"They were an odd pair. Ashurst still wore his uniform; but he seemed to have been rolling about in it on the ground; his sleek hair was wildly ruffled, and he was poking holes in the dust with his sword. Mackay had lost his topper, and wore a disreputable cap, his ancient frock-coat was without buttons, and his tie had worked itself up behind his ears. They talked excitedly to each other, now and then vouchsafing a scrap of information to an equally excited audience. When they saw me they rose and rushed for me, and dragged me between them up the street, while the crowd tailed at our heels.

"'Ye're a true prophet, Captain Thirlstone,' Mackay began, 'and I ask your pardon for doubting you. Ye said the Governor only needed a crisis to behave like a man. Well, the crisis has come; and if there's a man alive in this sinful world, it's that chief o' yours. And then his emotion overcame him. and, hard-bitten devil as he was, he sat down on the ground and gasped with hysterical laughter, while Ashurst, with a very red face, kept putting the wrong end of a cigarette in his mouth and swearing profanely.

"I never remember a madder sight. There was the brassy blue sky and reddish granite rock and acres of thick red dust. The scrub had that metallic greenness which you find in all copper places. Pretty unwholesome it looked, and the crowd, which had got round us again, was more unwholesome still. Fat Jew boys, with diamond rings on dirty fingers and greasy linen cuffs, kept staring at us with twitching lips; and one or two smarter fellows in riding-breeches, mine-managers and suchlike, tried to show their pluck by nervous jokes. And in the middle was Mackay, with his damaged frocker, drawling out his story in broad Scots.

"'He made this laddie put on his braws, and he commandeered this iniquitous garment for me. I've raxed its seams, and it'll never look again on the man that owns it. Syne he arrayed himself in purple and fine linen till he as like the king's daughter, all glorious without; and says he to me, "Mackay," he says, "we'll go and talk to these uncovenanted deevils in their own tongue. We'll visit them at home, Mackay," he says. "They're none such bad fellows, but they want a little humouring from men like you and me." So we got on our horses and started the procession--the Governor with his head in the air, and the laddie endenvouring to look calm and collected, and me praying to the God of Israel and trying to keep my breeks from working up above my knees. I've been in Kaffir wars afore, but I never thought I would ride without weapon of any kind into such a black Armageddon. I am a peaceable man for ordinar', and a canny one, but I wasna myself in that hour. Man, Thirlstone, I was that overcome by the spirit of your chief, that if he had bidden me gang alone on the same errand, I wouldna say but what Iwould have gone.

"'We hadna ridden half a mile before we saw the indunas and their men, ten thousand if there was one, and terrible as an army with banners. I speak feeguratively, for they hadna the scrap of a flag among them. They were beating the war-drums, and the young men were dancing with their big skin shields and wagging their ostrich feathers, so I saw they were out for business. I'll no' say but what my blood ran cold, but the Governor's eye got brighter and his back stiffer. "Kings may be blest," I says to myself, "but thou art glorious."

"'We rode straight for the centre of the crowd, where the young men were thickest and the big war-drums lay. As soon as they saw us a dozen lifted their spears and ran out to meet us. But they stopped after six steps. The sun glinted on the Governor's gold lace and my lum hat, and no doubt they thought we were heathen deities descended from the heavens. Down they went on their faces, and then back like rabbits to the rest, while the drums stopped, and the whole body awaited our coming in a silence like the tomb.

" Never a word we spoke, but just jogged on with our chins cocked up till we were forenent the big drum, where yon old scoundrel Umgazi was standing with his young men looking as black as sin. For a moment their spears were shaking in their hands, and I heard the click of a breech-bolt. If we had winked an eye we would have become pincushions that instant. But some unearthly power upheld us. Even the laddie kept a stiff face, and for me I forgot my breeks in watching the Governor. He looked as solemn as an archangel, and comes to a halt opposite Umgazi, where he glowers at the old man for maybe three minutes, while we formed up behind him. Their eyes fell before his, and by-and-by their spears dropped to their sides. "The father has come to his children," says he in their own tongue. "What do the children seek from their father?

"'Ye see the cleverness of the thing. The man's past folly came to help him. The natives had never seen the Governor before till they beheld him in gold lace and a cocked hat on a muckle horse, speaking their own tongue and looking like a destroying angel. I tell you the Labonga's knees were loosed under them. They durstna speak a word until the Governor repeated the question in the same quiet, steely voice. "You seek something," he said, "else you had not come out to meet me in your numbers. The father waits to hear the children's desires."

"'Then Umgazi found his tongue and began an uneasy speech. The mines, he said, truly enough, were the abode of devils, who compelled the people to work under the ground. The crops were unreaped and the buck went unspeared, because there were no young men left to him. Their father had been away or asleep, they thought, for no help had come from him; therefore it had seemed good to them, being freemen and warriors, to seek help for themselves.

"'The Governor listened to it all with a set face. Then he smiled at them with supernatural assurance. They were fools, he said, and people of little wit, and he flung the better part of the Book of Job at their heads. The Lord kens where the man got his uncanny knowledge of the Labonga. He had all their heathen customs by heart, and he played with them like a cat with a mouse. He told then they were damned rascals to make such a stramash, and damned fools to think they could frighten the white man by their demonstrations. There was no brag about his words, just a calm statement of fact. At the same time, he said, he had no mind to let any one wrong his children, and if any wrong had been done it should be righted. It was not meet, he said, that the young men should be taken from the villages unless by their own consent, though it was his desire that such young men as could be spared should have a chance of earning an honest penny. And then he fired at them some stuff about the British Empire and the King, and you could see the Labonga imbibing it like water. The man in a cocked hat might have told them that the sky was yellow, and they would have swallowed it.

"'I have spoken," he says at last, and there was a great shout from the young men, and old Umgazi looked pretty foolish. They were coming round our horses to touch our stirrups with their noses, but the Governor stopped them.

"'My children will pile their weapons in front of me." says he, " to show me how they have armed themselves, and likewise to prove that their folly is at an end. All except a dozen," says he, "whom I select as a bodyguard." And there and then he picked twelve lusty savages for his guard, while the rest without a cheep stacked their spears and guns forenent the big drum.

"'Then he turned to us and spoke in English. "Get back to the mines hell-for-leather, and tell them what's happening, and see that you get up some kind of a show for to-morrow at noon. I will bring the chiefs, and we'll feast them. Get all the bands you can, and let them play me in. Tell the mines fellows to look active for it's the chance of their lives. "Then he says to the Labonga, "My men will return he says, "but as for me I will spend the night with my children. Make ready food, but let no beer be made, for it is a solemn occasion."

"'And so we left him. I will not describe how I spent last night mysel', but I have something to say about this remarkable phenomenon. I could enlarge on the triumph of mind over matter. ....

"Mackay did not enlarge. He stopped, cocked his ears, and looked down the road, from which came the strains of 'Annie Laurie,' played with much spirit but grievously out of tune. Followed 'The British Grenadiers,' and then an attempt at 'The March of the Priests.' Mackay rose in excitement and began to crane his disreputable neck, while the band--a fine scratch collection of instruments--took up their stand at the end of the street, flanked by a piper in khaki who performed when their breath failed. Mackay chuckled with satisfaction. 'The deevils have entered into the spirit of my instructions,' he said. 'In a wee bit the place will be like Falkirk Tryst for din.

"Punctually at twelve there came a great hullabaloo up the road, the beating of drums and the yelling of natives, and presently the procession hove in sight. There was Tommy on his horse, and on each side of him six savages with feather head-dress, and shields and war-paint complete. After him trooped about thirty of the great chiefs, walking two by two, for all the world like an Aldershot parade. They carried no arms, but the bodyguard shook their spears, and let yells out of them that would have scared Julius Caesar. Then the band started in, and the piper blew up, and the mines people commenced to cheer, and I thought the heavens would fall. Long before Tommy came abreast of me I knew what I should see. His uniform looked as if it had been slept in, and his orders were all awry. But he had his head flung back, and his eyes very bright, and his jaw set square. He never looked to right or left, never recognised me or anybody, for he was seeing something quite different from the red road and the white shanties and the hot sky."

The fire had almost died out. Thirlstone stooped for a moment and stirred the peats.

"Yes," he said, "I knew that in his fool's ear the trumpets of all Asia were ringing, and the King of Bokhara was entering Samarkand."

BABYLON

(The Song of NEHEMIAH'S Workmen

How many miles to Babylon? 'Three score and ten. Can I get there by candle-light? Yes, and back again.

We are come back from Babylon, Out of the plains and the glare, To the little hills of our own country And the sting of our kindred air; To the rickle of stones on the red rock's edge Which Kedron cleaves like a sword. We will build the walls of Zion again, To the glory of Zion's lord.

Now is no more of dalliance By the reedy waters in spring, When we sang of home, and sighed, and dreamed, And wept on remembering. Now we are back in our ancient hills Out of the plains and the sun; But before we make it a dwelling-place There's a wonderful lot to be done.

The walls are to build from west to east, From Gihon to Olivet, Waters to lead and wells to clear, And the garden furrows to set. From the Sheep Gate to the Fish Gate Is a welter of mire and mess; And southward over the common lands 'Tis a dragon's wilderness.

The Courts of the Lord are a heap of dust Where the hill winds whistle and race, And the noble pillars of God His House Stand in a ruined place In the Holy of Holies foxes lair, And owls and night-birds build. There's a deal to do ere we patch it anew As our father Solomon willed.

Now is the day of the ordered life And the law which all obey. We toil by rote and speak by note And never a soul dare stray. Ever among us a lean old man Keepeth his watch and ward, Crying, "The Lord hath set you free: Prepare ye the way of the Lord."

A goodly task we are called unto, A task to dream on o' nights, --Work for Judah and Judah's God, Setting our lands to rights; Everything fair and all things square And straight as a plummet string. --Is it mortal guile, if once in a while Our thoughts go wandering?...

We were not slaves in Babylon, For the gate of our souls lay free, There in that vast and sunlit land On the edges of mystery. Daily we wrought and daily we thought, And we chafed not at rod and power, For Sinim, Ssabea, and dusky Hind Talked to us hour by hour.

The man who lives in Babylon May poorly sup and fare, But loves and lures from the ends of the earth Beckon him everywhere. Next year he too may have sailed strange seas And conquered a diadem; For kings are as common in Babylon As crows in Bethlehem.

Here we are bound to the common round In a land which knows not change Nothing befalleth to stir the blood Or quicken the heart to range; Never a hope that we cannot plumb Or a stranger visage in sight,-- At the most a sleek Samaritan Or a ragged Amorite.

Here we are sober and staid of soul, Working beneath the law, Settled amid our father's dust, Seeing the hills they saw. All things fixed and determinate, Chiselled and squared by rule; Is it mortal guile once in a while To try and escape from school?

We will go back to Babylon, Silently one by one, Out from the hills and the laggard brooks To the streams that brim in the sun. Only a moment, Lord, we crave, To breathe and listen and see.-- Then we start anew with muscle and thew To hammer trestles for Thee.

THE RIME OF TRUE THOMAS

X

THE TALE OF THE RESPECTABLE WHAUP AND THE GREAT GODLY MAN

This is a story that I heard from the King of the Numidians, who with his tattered retinue encamps behind the peat-ricks. If you ask me where and when it happened I fear that I am scarce ready with an answer. But I will vouch my honour for its truth; and if any one seek further proof, let him go east the town and west the town and over the fields of No mans land to the Long Muir, and if he find not the King there among the peat-ricks, and get not a courteous answer to his question, then times have changed in that part of the country, and he must continue the quest to his Majesty's castle in Spain.

Once upon a time, says the tale, there was a Great Godly Man, a shepherd to trade, who lived in a cottage among heather. If you looked east in the morning, you saw miles of moor running wide to the flames of sunrise, and if you turned your eyes west in the evening, you saw a great confusion of dim peaks with the dying eye of the sun set in a crevice. If you looked north, too, in the afternoon, when the life of the day is near its end and the world grows wise, you might have seen a country of low hills and haughlands with many waters running sweet among meadows. But if you looked south in the dusty forenoon or at hot midday, you saw the far-off glimmer of a white road, the roofs of the ugly little clachan of Kilmaclavers, and the rigging of the fine new kirk of Threepdaidle. It was a Sabbath afternoon in the hot weather, and the man had been to kirk all the morning. He had heard a grand sermon from the minister (or it may have been the priest, for I am not sure of the date and the King told the story quickly)--a fine discourse with fifteen heads and three parentheses. He held all the parentheses and fourteen of the heads in his memory, but he had forgotten the fifteenth; so for the purpose of recollecting it, and also for the sake of a walk, he went forth in the afternoon into the open heather.

The whaups were crying everywhere, making the air hum like the twanging of a bow. Poo-eelie, Poo-eelie, they cried, Kirlew, Kirlew, Whaup, Wha-up. Sometimes they came low, all but brushing him, till they drove settled thoughts from his head. Often had he been on the moors, but never had he seen such a stramash among the feathered clan. The wailing iteration vexed him, and he shoo'd the birds away with his arms. But they seemed to mock him and whistle in his very face, and at the flaff of their wings his heart grew sore. He waved his great stick; he picked up bits of loose moor-rock and flung them wildly; but the godless crew paid never a grain of heed. The morning's sermon was still in his head, and the grave words of the minister still rattled in his ear, but he could get no comfort for this intolerable piping. At last his patience failed him and he swore unchristian words. "Deil rax the birds' thrapples," he cried. At this all the noise was hushed and in a twinkling the moor was empty. Only one bird was left, standing on tall legs before him with its head bowed upon its breast, and its beak touching the heather.

Then the man repented his words and stared at the thing in the moss. "What bird are ye?" he asked thrawnly.

"I am a Respectable Whaup," said the bird, "and I kenna why ye have broken in on our family gathering. Once in a hundred years we foregather for decent conversation, and here we are interrupted by a muckle, sweerin' man."

Now the shepherd was a fellow of great sagacity, yet he never thought it a queer thing that he should be having talk in the mid-moss with a bird.

"What for were ye making siccan a din, then?" he asked. "D'ye no ken ye were disturbing the afternoon of the holy Sabbath?

The bird lifted its eyes and regarded him solemnly. "The Sabbath is a day of rest and gladness," it said, "and is it no reasonable that we should enjoy the like?"

The shepherd shook his head, for the presumption staggered him. "Ye little ken what ye speak of," he said. "The Sabbath is for them that have the chance of salvation, and it has been decreed that salvation is for Adam's race and no for the beasts that perish."

The whaup gave a whistle of scorn. "I have heard all that long ago. In my great grandmother's time, which 'ill be a thousand years and mair syne, there came a people from the south with bright brass things on their heads and breasts and terrible swords at their thighs. And with them were some lang gowned men who kenned the stars and would come out o' nights to talk to the deer and the corbies in their ain tongue. And one, I mind, foregathered with my great-grandmother and told her that the souls o' men flitted in the end to braw meadows where the gods bide or gaed down to the black pit which they ca' Hell. But the souls o' birds, he said, die wi' their bodies, and that's the end o' them. Likewise in my mother's time, when there was a great abbey down yonder by the Threepdaidle Burn which they called the House of Kilmaclavers, the auld monks would walk out in the evening to pick herbs for their distillings, and some were wise and kenned the ways of bird and beast. They would crack often o' nights with my ain family, and tell them that Christ had saved the souls o' men, but that birds and beasts were perishable as the dew o' heaven. And now ye have a black-gowned man in Threepdaidle who threeps on the same overcome. Ye may a' ken something o' your ain kitchen midden, but certes! ye ken little o' the warld beyond it."

Now this angered the man, and he rebuked the bird. "These are great mysteries," he said, "which are no to be mentioned in the ears of an unsanctified creature. What can a thing like you wi' a lang neb and twae legs like stilts ken about the next warld?"

"Weel, weel," said the whaup, "we'll let the matter be. Everything to its ain trade, and I will not dispute with ye on Metapheesics. But if ye ken something about the next warld, ye ken terrible little about this."

Now this angered the man still more, for he was a shepherd reputed to have great skill in sheep and esteemed the nicest judge of hogg and wether in all the countryside. "What ken ye about that?" he asked. "Ye may gang east to Yetholm and west to Kells, and no find a better herd."

"If sheep were a'," said the bird, "ye micht be right; but what o' the wide warld and the folk in it? Ye are Simon Etterick o' the Lowe Moss. Do ye ken aucht o' your forebears?"

"My father was a God-fearing man at the Kennelhead and my grandfather and great grandfather afore him. One o' our name, folk say, was shot at a dykeback by the Black Westeraw."

"If that's a'" said the bird, "ye ken little. Have ye never heard o' the little man, the fourth back from yoursel', who killed the Miller o' Bewcastle at the Lammas Fair? That was in my ain time, and from my mother I have heard o' the Covenanter who got a bullet in his wame hunkering behind the divot-dyke and praying to his Maker. There were others of your name rode in the Hermitage forays and turned Naworth and Warkworth and Castle Gay. I have heard o' an Etterick. Sim o' the Redcleuch, who cut the throat o' Jock Johnstone in his ain house by the Annan side. And my grandmother had tales o' auld Ettericks who rade wi' Douglas and the Bruce and the ancient Kings o' Scots; and she used to tell o' others in her mother's time, terrible shockheaded men hunting the deer and rinnin' on the high moors, and bidin' in the broken stane biggings on the hill-taps."

The shepherd stared, and he, too, saw the picture. He smelled the air of battle and lust and foray, and forgot the Sabbath.

"And you yoursel'," said the bird, "are sair fallen off from the auld stock. Now ye sit and spell in books, and talk about what ye little understand, when your fathers were roaming the warld. But little cause have I to speak, for I too am a downcome. My bill is two inches shorter than my mother's, and my grandmother was taller on her feet. The warld is getting weaklier things to dwell in it, even since I mind mysel'."

"Ye have the gift o' speech; bird," said the man, "and I would hear mair." You will perceive that he had no mind of the Sabbath day or the fifteenth head of the forenoon's discourse.

"What things have I to tell ye when ye dinna ken the very horn-book o' knowledge? Besides, I am no clatter-vengeance to tell stories in the middle o' the muir, where there are ears open high and low. There's others than me wi mair experience and a better skill at the telling. Our clan was well acquaint wi' the reivers and lifters o' the muirs, and could crack fine o' wars and the takin of cattle. But the blue hawk that lives in the corrie o' the Dreichil can speak o' kelpies and the dwarfs that bide in the hill. The heron, the lang solemn fellow, kens o' the greenwood fairies and the wood elfins, and the wild geese that squatter on the tap o' the Muneraw will croak to ye of the merry maidens and the girls o' the pool. The wren--him that hops in the grass below the birks--has the story of the Lost Ladies of the Land, which is ower auld and sad for any but the wisest to hear; and there is a wee bird bides in the heather-hill--lintie men call him--who sings the Lay of the West Wind, and the Glee of the Rowan Berries. But what am I talking of? What are these things to you, if ye have not first heard True Thomas's Rime, which is the beginning and end o' all things?"

"I have heard no rime" said the man, "save the sacred psalms o' God's Kirk."

"Bonny rimes" said the bird. "Once I flew by the hinder end o' the Kirk and I keekit in. A wheen auld wives wi' mutches and a wheen solemn men wi' hoasts! Be sure the Rime is no like yon."

"Can ye sing it, bird?" said the man, "for I am keen to hear it."

"Me sing!" cried the bird, "me that has a voice like a craw! Na, na, I canna sing it, but maybe I can tak ye where ye may hear it. When I was young an auld bogblitter did the same to me, and sae began my education. But are ye willing and brawly willing? --for if ye get but a sough of it ye will never mair have an ear for other music."

"I am willing and brawly willing," said the man.

"Then meet me at the Gled's Cleuch Head at the sun's setting," said the bird, and it flew away.

Now it seemed to the man that in a twinkling it was sunset, and he found himself at the Gled's Cleuch Head with the bird flapping in the heather before him. The place was a long rift in the hill, made green with juniper and hazel, where it was said True Thomas came to drink the water.

"Turn ye to the west," said the whaup, "and let the sun fail on your face; then turn ye five times round about and say after me the Rune Of the Heather and the Dew." And before he knew the man did as he was told, and found himself speaking strange words, while his head hummed and danced as if in a fever.

"Now lay ye down and put your ear to the earth," said the bird; and the man did so. Instantly a cloud came over his brain, and he did not feel the ground on which he lay or the keen hill-air which blew about him. He felt himself falling deep into an abysm of space, then suddenly caught up and set among the stars of heaven. Then slowly from the stillness there welled forth music, drop by drop like the clear falling of rain, and the man shuddered for he knew that he heard the beginning of the Rime.

High rose the air, and trembled among the tallest pines and the summits of great hills. And in it were the sting of rain and the blatter of hail, the soft crush of snow and the rattle of thunder among crags. Then it quieted to the low sultry croon which told of blazing midday when the streams are parched and the bent crackles like dry tinder. Anon it was evening, and the melody dwelled among the high soft notes which mean the coming of dark and the green light of sunset. Then the whole changed to a great paean which rang like an organ through the earth. There were trumpet notes ill it and flute notes and the plaint of pipes. "Come forth," it cried; "the sky is wide and it is a far cry to the world's end. The fire crackles fine o' nights below the firs, and the smell of roasting meat and wood smoke is dear to the heart of man. Fine, too is the sting of salt and the rasp of the north wind in the sheets. Come forth, one and all, unto the great lands oversea, and the strange tongues and the hermit peoples. Learn before you die to follow the Piper's Son, and though your old bones bleach among grey rocks, what matter if you have had your bellyful of life and come to your heart's desire?" And the tune fell low and witching, bringing tears to the eyes and joy to the heart; and the man knew (though no one told him) that this was the first part of the Rime, the Song of the Open Road, the Lilt of the Adventurer, which shall be now and ever and to the end of days.

Then the melody changed to a fiercer and sadder note. He saw his forefathers, gaunt men and terrible, run stark among woody hills. He heard the talk of the bronze-clad invader, and the jar and clangour as stone met steel. Then rose the last coronach of his own people, hiding in wild glens, starving in corries, or going hopelessly to the death. He heard the cry of the Border foray, the shouts of the famished Scots as they harried Cumberland, and he himself rode in the midst of them. Then the tune fell more mournful and slow, and Flodden lay before him. He saw the flower of the Scots gentry around their King, gashed to the breastbone, still fronting the lines of the south, though the paleness of death sat on each forehead. "The flowers of the Forest are gone," cried the lilt, and through the long years he heard the cry of the lost, the desperate, fighting for kings over the water and princes in the heather. "Who cares?" cried the air. "Man must die, and how can he die better than in the stress of fight with his heart high and alien blood on his sword? Heigh-ho! One against twenty, a child against a host, this is the romance of life." And the man's heart swelled, for he knew (though no one told him) that this was the Song of Lost Battles which only the great can sing before they die.

But the tune was changing, and at the change the man shivered for the air ran up to the high notes and then down to the deeps with an eldrich cry, like a hawk's scream at night, or a witch's song in the gloaming. It told of those who seek and never find, the quest that knows no fulfilment. "There is a road," it cried, "which leads to the Moon and the Great Waters. No changehouse cheers it, and it has no end; but it is a fine road, a braw road--who will follow it?" And the man knew (though no one told him) that this was the Ballad of Grey Weather, which makes him who hears it sick all the days of his life for something which he cannot name. It is the song which the birds sing on the moor in the autumn nights, and the old crow on the treetop hears and flaps his wing. It is the lilt which men and women hear in the darkening of their days, and sigh for the unforgettable; and love-sick girls get catches of it and play pranks with their lovers. It is a song so old that Adam heard it in the Garden before Eve came to comfort him, so young that from it still flows the whole joy and sorrow of earth.

THE MOON ENDURETH

Then it ceased, and all of a sudden the man was rubbing his eyes on the hillside, and watching the falling dusk. "I have heard the Rime," he said to himself, and he walked home in a daze. The whaups were crying, but none came near him, though he looked hard for the bird that had spoken with him. It may be that it was there and he did not know it, or it may be that the whole thing was only a dream; but of this I cannot say.

The next morning the man rose and went to the manse.

"I am glad to see you, Simon," said the minister, "for it will soon be the Communion Season, and it is your duty to go round with the tokens."

"True," said the man, "but it was another thing I came to talk about," and he told him the whole tale.

"There are but two ways of it, Simon," said the minister. "Either ye are the victim of witchcraft, or ye are a self-deluded man. If the former (whilk I am loth to believe), then it behoves ye to watch and pray lest ye enter into temptation. If the latter, then ye maun put a strict watch over a vagrant fancy, and ye'll be quit o' siccan whigmaleeries."

Now Simon was not listening but staring out of the window. "There was another thing I had it in my mind to say," said he. "I have come to lift my lines, for I am thinking of leaving the place."

"And where would ye go?" asked the minister, aghast.

"I was thinking of going to Carlisle and trying my luck as a dealer, or maybe pushing on with droves to the South."

"But that's a cauld country where there are no faithfu' ministrations," said the minister.

"Maybe so, but I am not caring very muckle about ministrations," said the man, and the other looked after him in horror.

When he left the manse he went to a Wise Woman, who lived on the left side of the kirkyard above Threepdaidle burn-foot. She was very old, and sat by the ingle day and night, waiting upon death. To her he told the same tale.

She listened gravely, nodding with her head. "Ach," she said, "I have heard a like story before. And where will you be going?"

"I am going south to Carlisle to try the dealing and droving" said the man, "for I have some skill of sheep."

"And will ye bide there?" she asked.

"Maybe aye, and maybe no," he said. "I had half a mind to push on to the big toun or even to the abroad. A man must try his fortune."

"That's the way of men," said the old wife. "I, too, have heard the Rime, and many women who now sit decently spinning in Kilmaclavers have heard it. But woman may hear it and lay it up in her soul and bide at hame, while a man, if he get but a glisk of it in his fool's heart, must needs up and awa' to the world's end on some daft-like ploy. But gang your ways and fare-ye-weel. My cousin Francie heard it, and he went north wi' a white cockade in his bonnet and a sword at his side, singing 'Charlie's come hame'. And Tam Crichtoun o' the Bourhopehead got a sough o' it one simmers' morning, and the last we heard o' Tam he was fechting like a deil among the Frenchmen. Once I heard a tinkler play a sprig of it on the pipes, and a' the lads were wud to follow him. Gang your ways for I am near the end o' mine."

And the old wife shook with her coughing. So the man put up his belongings in a pack on his back and went whistling down the Great South Road.

Whether or not this tale have a moral it is not for me to say. The King (who told it me) said that it had, and quoted a scrap of Latin, for he had been at Oxford in his youth before he fell heir to his kingdom. One may hear tunes from the Rime, said he, in the thick of a storm on the scarp of a rough hill, in the soft June weather, or in the sunset silence of a winter's night. But let none, he added, pray to have the full music; for it will make him who hears it a footsore traveller in the ways o' the world and a masterless man till death.

CPSIA information can be obtained
at www.ICGtesting.com
Printed in the USA
LVHW022306110620
657890LV00022B/3169